*Praise for Lauren C. Teffeau's*

# A HUNGER WITH NO NAME

"Lauren C. Teffeau's *A Hunger with No Name* is a powerful story of survival—personal, ecological, and cultural—in the presence of over-whelming technological power. The textures and politics of Teffeau's world are so finely wrought, the relationships so carefully crafted, that I could almost taste the starlight and feel every connection and disconnection. A powerful and important story filled with mystery and heart."

—Fran Wilde, Nebula-winning author of *Updraft* and the Gemworld series

"A heartfelt coming of age story about a girl made of starways and ancient stories who must decide what matters when her people and their way of life face annihilation. A reminder to us all of what it means to be human and in community and how far one girl will go to save her world. A thought-provoking meditation on what is lost and what is gained when we rely on technology to save us."

—*New York Times* best-selling author Rebecca Roanhorse

"A powerful environmental fable with a headstrong heroine, Teffeau's tale of a nomadic desert people forced into a high-tech city offers a glimpse into a unique fantasy world, and a testimony to the crucial cultural impact of storytelling."

—Sarena Ulibarri, author of *Another Life*

# A HUNGER WITH NO NAME

Lauren C. Teffeau

UNIVERSITY OF TAMPA PRESS
POMME

Manufactured in the United States of America
First Edition

On the Cover: "Star of the Hero" by Nicolas Roerich, 1936. Courtesy of Nicholas Roerich Museum, New York.

Cover design by Madeline M. Eisele

The University of Tampa Press
401 West Kennedy Boulevard
Tampa, FL 33606

This is a work of fiction. Unless otherwise indicated, all the names, characters, businesses, places, events, and incidents in this book are either the product of the author's imagination or used in a fictitious manner. Any resemblance to actual persons, living or dead, or actual events is purely coincidental.

ISBN 978-1-59732-206-5 (pbk.)
ISBN 978-1-59732-207-2 (hbk.)
ISBN 978-1-59732-208-9 (ebook)

Library of Congress Control Number:
2024932802

Browse & order online at
utampapress.org

*For my daughter Brynn—*
*May you always shine brightly.*

# A HUNGER WITH NO NAME

# TABLE OF CONTENTS

## I. The Impulsive One

I find the very last water cache as the sun touches the horizon, painting the Glass City far to the north red and gold. The last person through the waystation didn't set the marking stones properly, making it harder to find in the fading light with the day's work weighing down my shoulders.

Crouching, I keep my back to the Glass City only in part so its glow won't spoil my vision. Inside the dugout, three clay vessels roughly the size of a child's head are full of life-giving water. The fourth's been smashed, the braided reed stopper the only thing salvageable. I pluck it from the jagged shards and pull another vessel from my pack, already stoppered and tied loosely with twine. I nestle it with the others, insulate each one with dirt, then drape sticks and twigs over the hole, before topping it over with more sandy dirt.

The marking stones are the last step. Five round stones, palm-sized, dark and smooth from handling except for the constellations carved into each one to represent the cache's location relative to the stars.

When I rise to my feet, Mother's walking the perimeter, our herd of lucerva mewling and blowing and stamping their hooves, eager to be off. We have a long night of travel ahead of us if we want to reach Astrava by morning. "Replaced a vessel in the cache to the southwest," I call to her. "It didn't have the right markings either."

She reaches my side and tsks. "Lose your place in the stars, you lose more than your way."

"I fixed it, but why not mind our own water stores instead of refilling these caches? Others are never as careful." And it's been happening more and more frequently of late.

"Waystations are a traveler's only hope through the desert," she says. "We respect those who've been through here before and those who come after by ensuring the caches are full lest *we* be the ones without next time."

At the implied rebuke, I shrink into the thick lucerva fur lining my cloak.

Mother nods to the nearest lucerva. "We can always replace the vessel when we return to Astrava." And the animals' birthing grounds. "May we always afford to be so generous," she adds softly.

Lucerva have been a friend to Astravans for generations. I don't need to tell Mother how the herd grows smaller each year thanks to nazoph attacks and sick yeanlings who never seem to gain their footing on the lean terrain. Outcomes surely writ in the stars, but that doesn't make their passing any easier to bear.

Would that the world be as generous to us if our lucerva continue to dwindle.

Mother whistles to Rakravat. He returns a series of short tones from the back of the herd. As we march home under the cover of starlight, he'll keep an eye out for stragglers. From the east toward the front, Linarv replies with a snippet from an old caravan song, its high-pitched tune said to bring good luck and keep the sky clear of monsters. He and Mother will trade off leading the herd home. She waits a few minutes longer, for the stars to brighten, secure in their place in the night sky, before she whistles again for us to be off.

The herd lurches into movement, Mother and I walking alongside the four-legged animals. The fully-grown ones reach our waists. Twin horns curve along either side of their heads like a bony crown. I sink my fingers into the pelt of the closest lucerva, the scratchy top fur giving way to downy warmth underneath.

"Tell me, what is that one?"

I follow the line of Mother's staff, pointing to a cluster of stars to the southeast, and swallow a burst of annoyance. "The Impulsive One, doomed to always seek and never find."

She doesn't reward me with a smile or empty words of praise. Navigating the desert is much too important for that, even if there's nothing left for me to learn. "And that one?"

This time it's a thin line of stars with three larger ones making a triangular point at the end. "The Laborer, of course. Endless toil, rewarded only by their proximity to the Joyful One." That's a constellation of seven stars in a radiant spiral, immediately next to the shovel-shaped formation.

Mother tests me until she's satisfied by my command of the constellations. Needlessly because I make no mistakes, but perhaps she isn't doing it for my sake. "The stars see fit to shine down on us, this last night of the graze," she finally says.

No clouds in the sky, the air so crisp it burns my lungs with each inhale. "At least there's that."

Even though it doesn't seem like the stars have seen fit to bless much else of our graze—the months we spend traveling the desert so our herd goes into the birthing season as healthy as possible. Too little vitav, the quick-growing creepers that sprout from a river running deep underground throughout the region, and hardly any surface lichen covering stones and scrubby tree trunks that the lucervas' thick tongues strip bare, turning their thin frames bulky for our return to Astrava.

Mother's staff thunks beside me, sinking into the sandy ground with each step. A gangly yeanling squawks indignantly when it gets too close. "What troubles you, little one?"

I don't know how to answer. A sense of futility seems to cloud our work with the animals. The work of Mother's mother and her mother before her. From a young age, I've known how to shear their bristly coats, clean their clawed hooves, and apply salve created from the vitav we collect to protect their skin during the days of long sun. Mother did *not* teach me how to watch them die. That was something we learned together as the lands our people traveled for generations continue to wither up around us, leaving us stranded along the barren wastes with only the Glass City shining in the distance.

But voicing my concerns feels wrong. Ungrateful even. "The herd will finish out this season well enough. But what about the next one? One bad breeding season and—"

"Don't say it."

"But the Glass City—"

Mother whirls toward me. I fall silent as the lucerva mill around us, confused by our actions. Her jaw works for a moment, then she resumes the pace, the herd following her movements. I can only do the same.

The elders say the Glass City changes people. All those reflective surfaces, all the lights that shine straight into your mind and corrupt the soul. We aren't even supposed to look at it winking on the horizon, lest it tempt us. But without a strong herd, Mother and I won't be able to ignore the call of the city for long. Nor would the rest of Astrava. We've already lost too many to its glistening walls.

Mother remains quiet except for the tapping of her staff over the rocky terrain, so long I nearly give up hope of a response. "You see much, little one," she finally says. "I hoped to keep such possibilities from you a little longer, but there's no cause for worry. Things may yet turn around. May the stars make it so."

My boot scuffs against a stone, and I tamp down the urge to give it a kick. It would only upset the animals.

Mother gives me a sidelong glance. "Once, the stars were richer and more numerous than they are now. So many, it was hard to keep track of them all. Over time, they faded—some gone in the blink of an eye. Others blazed furiously, filing the sky with the heat of their indignation. But their waning made room in the sky for the stars that remained to shine to their fullest. The very stars that have guided our people for generations."

I know the rest: how once our people weren't confined to navigate the stars by foot. They created vessels that flew through the air, floating over dunes and scrub, eyes always to the sky, along with other marvelous things. But then, as always, war cast them across the world like seeds carelessly strewn to sprout where they landed. Some groups survived the Great Scatter, some didn't, but all struggled to rebuild what they once had. Our people have been earthbound ever since, confined to a territory bordered by the Rask Mountains to the northwest and the Dentand range to the east. We tamed the lucerva, and now we travel the desert and trade with the clans of the Karnez to the south.

But anything beyond that is out of reach, including the stars.

"Yet we're merely surviving. How can you call this shining to the fullest?"

Mother hisses. Her face is hidden by the rough spun scarf wrapped around her head to stay warm, but I can imagine her expression. A tightening of the delicate skin around her dark brown eyes and mouth, the determined jut of her pointed chin.

"And sometimes," Mother goes on stubbornly, picking back up the thread of her story, "the stars burned so brightly, for so long, we couldn't tell they were fading. So slow, so steady their decline, we didn't notice until they were gone. We all have a choice, Thurava. To give up, to destroy, or to go on the best we can. Astravans have always tried to be the slow-dying star—may you never live to see its end. But even if you do, we do not turn aside. We do not turn away. We bear witness in respect to all that has come before."

"Yes, Mother." So thoroughly chastened, it's the only thing I can say. Our future is written in the stars. All that's left is for us to live it.

We reach Astrava before the full force of dawn. The settlement spreads out along the western bank of the Najimov at the point where the high desert recedes and scrubby grassland takes over. A view that makes my heart sigh no matter how many times I see it.

Our arrival's heralded by lookouts wielding lucerva horns, a deep sound that buzzes through my sternum. Shouts of welcome rise with the sun, and cookfires are coaxed into blazing. Rakravat leads forth a prancing male tossing his head proudly who'll be harvested for the meal to celebrate our homecoming. Despite our exhaustion, we'll feast and share news of the graze, in turn learning all that transpired while we were away.

Kikriva rushes over, securing a clean work apron around her waist as she nears. Her curly brown hair's been hastily pulled into a plait at the back of her head. Her brother Zurlot, still chubby with baby fat, trots behind her. "We hoped you'd return today." She gives me a quick hug, heedless of the road dust clinging to me. "Come, let us help you."

Mother, Linarv, and Rakravat have already gone off with other friends and neighbors to freshen up from our journey. As I rub grit from my eyes, Kikriva ushers me toward her family's pavilion. Her brother clutches the hem of my cloak to keep up with us.

Waterproofed lucerva hides cover the wooden structure built a few feet off the ground. The only exception is a small flap near the center of the roof that can be pulled back to reveal the stars. Inside, it's still cozy warm. I shrug out of my cloak and take a seat on the hide-strewn floor. My aching feet welcome the rest. Zendava, Kikriva's mother, bundles me into her arms. Then she deftly picks through my thick brown hair and braids it while Kikriva wipes away the dirt on my face and hands. Zurlot tries to feed me berries that grow along the riverbank, his mouth purple with ones he's already purloined from the bowl, but I wave him off. My appetite will wait for the feast.

"You have my thanks," I say.

"And our thanks to you," Kikriva's mother replies as is custom. "A good graze?"

I give her a hesitant nod. "Better than last year." Despite my fears, that much is true.

"That *is* good news," Zendava says as she ties off one of the braids.

LAUREN C. TEFFEAU

Clean and refreshed, I can finally focus on Kikriva who's practically vibrating with repressed emotion. "And how have things been here?"

Her brown eyes, shining like flecks of mica, widen. "We've had visitors from the Glass City." Her mother hisses. "What? They'll find out soon enough."

Zendava relinquishes her hold on my hair and faces me once more. "We're grateful for your family's safe return, Thurava." She moves to leave the pavilion but not before giving her daughter a warning look. "I'll see you at the feast. Don't be late."

Kikriva watches her go then turns back to me eagerly. "They brought us more books, and one of their clockwork creatures has been staying here to teach us their language."

"Mother will be furious when she finds out."

The Glass City didn't always dominate the horizon. Once, its people were content to live off the land like Astravans. But something changed, and they began building. At first, we thought they wanted to get closer to the stars. But as the city grew bigger and brighter, it became clear they were more interested in escaping the land. Construction razed the ground, trees and vegetation uprooted or smothered by dirt and rock. Smoke and strange clouds crawled through the air, inexorably drifting closer to Astrava. Years of negotiations between the Astravan elders and the Glass City's metallic liaisons halted the worst of it when I was younger.

But the land still hasn't recovered. And the harder things get in Astrava, the easier it becomes to turn toward the Glass City for a fresh start.

Kikriva brings me a stack of books. "I read these while you were away." She sets a handful aside and puts the others in Zurlot's hands. "Take these to Thurava's pavilion, please." Her attention returns to me. "I selected the most interesting for you."

Zurlot goes outside, leaving the two of us alone. "What do you have for me this time?" Before I was old enough to go on the graze with Mother, I stayed with Kikriva's family those long months the herd was away. Kikriva and I often read the same book, trading off chapters so neither of us could get too far ahead of the other. But the graze changed all that. Now, I must trust Kikriva's judgment of what books are worth my time. Luckily, she knows me well.

"Another volume of the histories, an account of the Great Navigator's travels, and one book that came from the Glass City itself."

"I'm not so sure Mother will approve."

Kikriva shrugs. "What does it matter? Your mind's your own. Books won't change that." She squeezes my shoulders in a spontaneous hug. I've missed her so. "Besides, I need you to read them so I finally have someone to talk to about what they say."

The elders never quite knew what to do about our interest in books, as the other children were happy to not spend all their free time with musty tomes, fragile and in some cases incomplete from so much handling over the years. Though having more books to choose from is welcome, as we've exhausted Astrava's stores many times over. Even if they do come from the Glass City.

"And what do they say?" I ask.

She brightens. "Did you know you don't have to wear animal fur or roughspun in the city? Their clothes are so soft and slippery, it's like wearing air."

"That's what you want? To wear nothing at all?" I tease.

Kikriva starts. "What? No. But can you imagine? The things possible there . . . It's as though the age before has come again."

Before the Great Scatter brought darkness to the world. But the Glass City, a star in ascendance? The elders have always maintained the city's out of balance with its surroundings. They didn't even consult with the stars, placing it along the path of Serpent's Fork, the twisting constellation symbolizing two equally bad choices. Yet I suppose a bad choice is better than no choice.

"Just think, Thurava—" A horn blast calling us to join the rest of the villagers at the feast silences Kikriva.

We leave the pavilion and hasten to the cookfires. Already the scent of roasting meat and baking bread fill the air. I crane my neck, hoping for a glimpse of the metallic creature sent here from the Glass City. A flash of light places the liaison alongside the elders' pavilion where the business of the settlement is conducted. One of our history books discussed such strange machines made of clockwork and metal, running on a source of energy that doesn't come from wind or water or fire.

Mother's always resisted the other elders' insistence on calling it magic, saying it gives the Glass City liaisons too much power when there's another word for it, lost in the Great Scatter. But her leaving for the graze makes it difficult to win such arguments. She's told me more than once she feels like the Truthteller, a set of stars to the north, in that she always speaks honestly but is never believed by the others.

Kikriva worries her lower lip. "Thurava, there's something you should know."

I come to a stop, and she does too. These homecomings are always so strange as my memory of Kikriva collides with who she is now, with so many months between us. But even still, there's a look in her eyes I'm certain wasn't there when we left for the graze. "What is it?"

"The liaison's offered to bring us to the city."

The longing in her voice kindles my suspicions. Whenever we're in Astrava, I can feel the Glass City—a slight pressure like the predatory gaze of a nazoph from the underbrush. In my time away, Kikriva must have looked at the city and given into the temptation of envisioning another life. "You cannot leave," I say sharply. "What about your family's work?"

She waves that off. "Anyone can prepare a hide." That's true, but for her to express such disdain is a slap to the face. "My cousin's been training under Father for years. They could take over."

They could, but not easily. Kikriva's family has been tanning the hides of lucerva for as long as mine's been herding them. They are masters at shaping lucerva hide into clothing, tools, and household supplies, fitting function to form. Invaluable techniques that will be lost if her family leaves for the Glass City.

Her gaze turns worried. "Don't look so alarmed. Nothing's been decided yet."

"Decided?" As if it's some choice freely made and not a betrayal of all we know?

She hunches her shoulders. "What do you want me to say?"

"You're actually considering it?"

If I wasn't certain earlier, I am now. How could my best friend, a sister in so many ways, think to leave all this—*me*—behind? Mother's always said the hardest part about being a herder is that life goes on at Astrava while we track our charges through the desert. Something I've never really faced in my sixteen years until this moment.

"There you are." Fracturing my standoff with Kikriva, Mother looks refreshed with her thick brown hair brushed to gleaming, her tan cheeks rosy with good humor, completely at ease now that we're back home. She gives Kikriva a quick hug. "I should have known you two would be together." After an apologetic nod at Kikriva, Mother leads me over to where the other elder council members have gathered along with the most high, a sun-darkened old man with hair like thistledown, deemed to be the wisest elder in Astrava.

Numbly, I sit down with Mother on my right side and Linarv, looking well with his reddish beard trimmed, on my left. Next to him is Rakravat with his glossy black hair neatly parted. They both dislike the ceremony and the attention that always accompanies our return to Astrava, but they do what they must for Mother's sake.

We all do.

She tries to hide her preoccupation as the first platters are passed around the fire, but I can see her gaze flick toward the elders' pavilion, the spindly form of our Glass City visitor watching on. Her frame vibrates with disapproval, but she still smiles through her greetings with the other council members.

The most high asks for Mother's report once she's eaten a few ceremonial bites. "We lost two adult lucerva to nazoph," she says, "but over half the females are pregnant."

That's more than last year. Around the campfire, cheers break out at such good fortune.

"We spoke with a trader from Karnez." The people to the south. "A string of bad luck has made them desperate for more bone fertilizer. That'll be a way to replenish our stores of dried fruit."

The elders nod approvingly at that. The most high raises a cup and salutes Mother, then both Linarv and Rakravat. "Thank you, Sitarva, daughter of Vachava, for another successful graze. The stars have seen fit to shine down on all of us thanks to your efforts."

A fresh loaf of bread is pulled back from the coals and passed around. I rip off a hunk to sop up the heavily spiced sauce that always accompanies the greens.

I try to catch Kikriva's eye across the fire, but she avoids my gaze. Her parents look subdued as they talk in low voices to their neighbors. That cannot bode well. Part of me wants to scream in frustration, but the feast's a time of celebration. I cannot spoil it.

Dish after dish go around the fire, with stories to accompany each one. I relish in the food, so much more elaborate than what we can manage when we're away from Astrava, but I grow impatient for the end of the meal. Bellies full, people start breaking away in twos and threes. Rakravat and Linarv make their excuses as well, doing a poor job of hiding their relief at leaving.

"When did the liaison arrive?" Mother asks the most high once enough people have cleared away to give them privacy.

"One month into your journey."

Once, when the liaisons came to Astrava with their food and supplies and books, the elders welcomed their generosity. That was when the first family left for the glistening city on the horizon, with promises not to forget Astrava or the life we've all created here.

When they weren't heard from again, whispers started at how the family had never been content with their lot, always hungering for what they couldn't have, no wonder they left, and good riddance. But as other families followed in the intervening years and only silence was left in their wake, we blamed the city for swallowing them up and spitting them out as strangers.

Now liaisons are a stark reminder of what's been lost. And what's still at risk. My gaze goes to Kikriva as she and her family leave the feast without a backward glance.

Mother hisses. "The liaison's been here this whole time?"

The most high nods slowly. "It brought us metal for Bravlat." The settlement's toolmaker. A most precious gift. Mother's face turns to the stone Bravlat often works. "Books too. It only asked to teach its language to anyone who was interested. There's more, but—" The most high's milky blue gaze cuts to me.

Her mouth has a grim set to it when she says, "Thurava, go to our pavilion. You're nearly asleep."

"I am not," I reply, indignant.

"I won't tell you again," Mother says, sharply this time.

Council business, it must be, but the dismissal stings. I roll to my feet, barely keeping my bow civil as I turn away from the fire. But before I return to the pavilion I share with Mother, I travel the path through waist-high scrub to the Najimov. Having watered this settlement for generations, the river deserves our respect. In the late morning sun, it's a sight that should bring warmth to my heart. Instead, cold dread fills me as it did the night before. I hadn't seen it for what it was at the time, thinking it only the desert chill.

When I was younger, the river ran vibrant blue. Depending on the season, it roared by or slowed to a narrow stream. But now, it only ever trickles, sometimes smelling foul or full of reddish-orange sediment that forces us to rely on water caches until the Najimov runs clearer. Mother and some of the elders think it's the work of the Glass City upriver, but they cannot prove it, not with the headwaters located well beyond Astravan territory. For now, enough water comes through to support the settlement, but never enough to thrive. A delicate balance, that—may it not worsen in the years to come.

In the blazing sunlight, the city's almost unbearable to look at. With a grimace, I turn away, but I can feel the weight of its reach, prickling along the back of my neck.

A shock of night air rips me from sleep as my blankets are tugged away. Kikriva resolves out of the darkness, a small lantern resting on the floor beside my bed. The apprehension on her face pulls any remaining drowsiness from my mind as I sit up. Mother's steady breaths buffet the curtain separating our sleeping platforms. Thankfully, she always sleeps like the dead after a graze.

Kikriva takes my hand and squeezes—urgently—and I realize what's so wrong about this moment. "You're leaving." I mean to be accusing, but I sound merely tired. And I am, despite sleeping most of the day since the feast.

She nods solemnly, though even now, I can see the excited hunger in her gaze. "Father says we'll be able to start over at the Glass City," she whispers back. "Think of it. No more sand in our eyes or stink of lucerva dung." They do not stink to me. "No more campfires," she goes on, "no more scrubbing hides, no more simply *reading* about things."

When I remain silent, Kikriva gives me a bittersweet smile. "I'm not like you. I have tanners' hands, forever doomed to stay behind." Being a herder allows me to travel, see the world beyond Astrava, that much is true. It doesn't matter to Kikriva that it's mostly desert—I get to leave, and she cannot. "I want to do things. There, I'll have a chance."

A lump forms in my throat. Kikriva's spoken her truth, and I cannot argue with it. Growing up, we both read the epic tales of the stars overhead that guide our people, but Kikriva's always acted like the Impulsive One, her interests fickle and ever-changing to make up for a lifetime of monotonous work. I hope she can find what she's looking for in the Glass City.

"We waited until you returned so I could say goodbye." Tears glimmer in Kikriva's eyes but don't fall. "I won't be like the others, though. I'll send word where you can find me. Perhaps—"

She cuts that thought off, unwilling to pledge more than she can give. Astravans never make a promise they cannot keep. I squeeze my friend's hands, and we sit like that for a long moment until Mother murmurs to herself as she rolls over. She still slumbers, but it's a reminder we're running out of time.

"I must go," Kikriva whispers brokenly.

And I must let her. "May the stars shine down on you," I say as she slips away into the night.

## II. The Laborer

When I greet the morning the next day, the entire village is already awake. Did I sleep so late? I push back the flaps of our pavilion and find the sun's barely cleared the Dentand Mountains.

"There you are." Mother strides over. "It pains me to tell you this, but Kikriva's family and two others left for the Glass City sometime in the night." That explains everyone's unease so early this morn, their faces full of apprehension and no little anger. The hurt flares once more before I quench it. Mother studies me, her mouth not quite a frown. "This doesn't surprise you?" She cups my cheek, her fingertips finding salt trails from last night's tears.

I wipe them away with my sleeve. "Kikriva told me."

"Hmm." Mother steps back, gathering her robes closer to her frame. At her forbidding look, I dare not waste any more time and join the others around the fire.

The most high waves to the crowd for quiet. "We're saddened to learn of three families' departures last night. Just as it was their choice to leave for the Glass City—" A number of people hiss at the mere mention of our neighbor to the north. "—it's *our* choice how to carry on without them." I marvel at how such a deep voice can come from such a frail frame. But the most high's always wielded his words well in his service to the stars. He looks us over and raises his arms to the sky. "A new day for all of us."

Someone shouts a question about how leather goods will be made now that Kikriva's family is gone.

"We'll do what we always do. Appoint a new master leatherworker for the village."

He turns, no doubt intent for the sanctuary of the elder's pavilion, as dismayed chatter breaks out. A new master leatherworker certainly, probably Kikriva's cousin as she herself suggested, but without her father to guide and train them? The way forward for whoever's chosen won't be easy.

Mother's hand on my elbow stays me when I turn for home. "You should have told me."

"I only learned of it last night."

Her eyes widen. "We could have stopped them."

"And what?" I ask before I can think better of it. "Ask them to reconsider when they'd already chosen a path forward?" Kikriva's explanations still don't sit well with me, but I cannot deny she wants what Astrava cannot give her. Would that it be otherwise. Then she'd be here still.

"I know Kikriva was your friend . . . "

"She still is." Her leaving won't change that. She said as much.

Mother's face softens. "Just remember how their decision hurt Astrava this day. That will be hard to forget." She turns and faces the glimmer on the horizon with a scowl. "Or forgive."

And yet they did it anyway, knowing the toll it would take on Astrava. Not something that was decided lightly as Kikriva attested.

"Where are you going?" Mother asks me when I take a step back.

"I haven't eaten yet. I'll meet you at the lucerva pens."

Reluctantly, she lets me go. "Bravlat should have sharpened our shears for us," she calls after me. "Pick them up on your way."

I dash back to our pavilion to scrub my face and eat a small breakfast of berries and leftover bread from yesterday's feast. There's one other thing I must do before seeing to Mother's errand.

When I reach the elders' pavilion, the entrance is drawn tightly closed, and a small curl of red smoke drifts through the flap in the roof. A meeting's in session. I wonder if Mother knows. I then dash that thought because I'm certain she wouldn't be happy to know why I'm here in the first place.

I approach the liaison stationed alongside the pavilion. Mother's always said the liaisons are nothing more than carrion birds picking over a dead carcass. "But that means we've already passed on if the liaisons are just fighting over scraps," I replied once. Mother gave me a startled look and pulled me into a hug. She told me not to worry, that we'd do as we've always done, tending the lucerva and keeping the herd well-grazed and watered. When an animal passes, we harvest fur, hide, meat, and bone. What's left over, we burn, our offering to the stars watching over us.

Mother always told me it would be enough.

The liaison straightens slightly when it notices me, and its eyes swirl to life like black ink written across a mirror. It's taller than Rakravat though not as broad. A clicking sound rattles through its chest.

"You're in contact with the Glass City?"

It considers me with its strange, unblinking eyes. "Yes, I am."

"Then you'll be able to tell me when Kikriva and the others reach its walls, yes?"

A shallow nod. "Yes. I will know when they reach Miravat."

That's the true name of the Glass City, but I, like most Astravans, avoid using it whenever possible. Bad luck, the elders have always said, but that wasn't enough to keep Kikriva's family away.

"And you'll be able to give them a message?"

"That is not the primary purpose for my connection to the city."

"But you could do it," I press.

It nods again, this time more formally, an unintended mockery of the gesture. "I will, for you, Thurava of Astrava."

I step back in surprise. "How do you know my name?"

"I know the name of every Astravan here." It spreads its spindly hands, each comprised of two joint-less fingers and a pincher-like thumb, toward the pavilions beyond, terracing the bluffs overlooking the Najimov. "The other children are eager to talk to me."

Did their incautious chatter give the liaison information on the whole village or had it learned all this by watching us these past weeks? Mother will be unhappy to learn of its observations regardless of how they were gained.

"I am here to help, Thurava of Astrava."

Unease crawls down my spine. Backing away with a muttered thanks, I quickly make my way to Bravlat. I don't want Mother wondering what kept me. The liaison seems to watch me the whole way until I reach the workstalls and finally pass out of view.

Bravlat greets me with a grin when he looks up from his bench. "Ah, Thurava. I've been expecting you." Gray peppers his temples and beard, his brown forearms brawny with muscle and spattered with shiny dark scars. He walks over to the wall where all sorts of tools and implements are hung, the better to see them all. "I've readied your old shears and made you a new set as well." He hands them over to me with pride, the metal blades gleaming.

"You're much too kind. I'll let Mother know about the second pair, and we'll find a way to repay you."

"Nonsense. What's good for the lucerva is good for Astrava, eh?"

I cannot help smiling at that. "Still. You have our thanks."

He waves me off and settles back down at his bench, humming to himself.

When I reach the pens, I pat the shears in my cloak's pocket. The jingle perks the ears of the older lucerva grazing nearby. They trot over, jostling each other for the privilege to be rid of their heavy coats first. More lucerva join them, some merely curious at the commotion, others eager to be shaved too. A task that takes at least a week to get through them all, but there's no telling the animals not to rush.

When Mother joins me at midday, my knees and back ache. I finish shearing a full-grown female, her belly already swollen with new life, and gladly take a break. Mother sits with me as we eat grain cakes and hard cheese and listen to the animals stamp and snort and shuffle about. A hawk soars overhead. The birds that nest along the river halt their song until it passes. A breeze scented with flowers and water vapor takes the bite out of the sun streaming down. I've already sweated through my undertunic, and the season of long sun's barely begun.

Mother sighs contentedly. There's a stillness to everything when we're back in Astrava that we can never find when we're on the graze. There's simply too much to do. But here, we can take our rest without worrying what comes next and simply soak in our surroundings.

At least for a little while.

The sun shines longer and hotter with each passing day. Too hot for even Linarv to sing. When it seems like the very earth should boil underneath the naked sun, it's time. We isolate the pregnant females. The rest of the herd will spend their time grazing in the outer fields while we wait for the yeanlings to make their appearance. Mother has an uncanny sense for which one will arrive first, barking orders to me, Linarv, and Rakravat as we make ready to welcome them. The new arrivals greet us with wobbly limbs and mewling cries. We clean them up, each of us taking turns handling them so they can learn our scents, and nestle them against their exhausted mothers' sides to nurse. For the next week, we sleep in shifts so someone's always on hand while the yeanlings learn the new world they've been brought into.

The stars shine down on us when none are stillborn or die in the days that follow.

One morning, instead of dashing to the yeanling pen first thing, I drop off the books Kikriva borrowed on my behalf. The assembled elders halt their discussion at my arrival at their pavilion. I give them a short bow of greeting. "I'm sorry. I didn't see the smoke so I assumed—"

"It's all right, Thurava, dear," the most high says, beckoning me closer. His sweeping gaze touches on the others. "We were about to call a meeting."

"Oh. I'll be sure to tell Mother when I see her."

"Don't bother," Rakravat's aunt says from her place in the circle. "She removed herself from this topic long ago."

The most high raises a hand, and Janeeva falls silent, though her green eyes are still bright with something suspiciously like malice.

I've no desire to be caught up in Mother's uneasy history with the council. I set the books on the shelf near the entrance and return outside.

The liaison glints in the morning light. "Greetings, Thurava of Astrava."

"Any news from Kikriva?" The same question I ask every time I've seen it these past long weeks.

"Her family made it safely to Miravat 43 days ago," it responds in a monotone voice.

"But no message?" I press.

"No message."

I swallow my disappointment. Perhaps something's happened, some kind of delay, making it difficult for Kikriva to send word. I must trust she'll reach out when she can.

The liaison watches me with its unblinking eyes. "Is there anything else I—"

I'm already stalking toward the lucerva pens, my light summer cloak flapping behind me.

The yeanlings' progress is our guide for the days to come. When they're ready to face the desert, so will we all. Their spindly forms fill out, and they range farther and farther away from their mothers' protection each day.

Linarv watches them with me one afternoon, noting which ones are fearless, which ones watch the others before making their move, asking me what I've observed as they've transformed from the fuzzy affectionate creatures I could hold in my arms to the tufted rambunctious terrors they've become. The long nights of travel will help with some of that, but it's better to know the personalities of the new arrivals now before they're tested by the graze.

"What of that one, Thurava?" Linarv points out a male yeanling with a dark brown stripe along its back.

"Oh, that one. He's into everything."

Linarv grunts. "How's he with the others?"

"He was the first to wean and often leads the others into trouble."

"Smart and curious. A difficult combination." Linarv frowns. "We'll make sure he spends time with the older males and see if that tempers him."

We go back to watching. Linarv isn't prone to chitchat. We could spend all afternoon here and not say a spare word, and that would be fine with both of us. He takes his obligations to the Laborer seriously, but I secretly think he has the soul of a poet. Unrecognizable from the man he was a few years ago, branded a troublemaker, his days full of fights and drunkenness. When his helpmate died, his grief was a wild, destructive thing the rest of Astrava was ill-equipped to handle.

He would have been cast out if Mother hadn't intervened and brought him into the fold. But his pain echoed her own when Father died. The only thing that kept her from expressing it in the same way, she says, was me. Though I suspect it was actually her obligations to the herd.

Linarv points out a few other difficult yeanlings, his trained eyes missing nothing as they continue their play, then falls back into a serious sort of silence.

Mother told me once she feared Linarv viewed his work with the lucerva as penance for his past instead of a new start. That would explain his melancholy air at times, but not his joy and pride at working with the animals. Or the rest of us.

But as all Astravans know, the Joyful One wasn't always joyful. Perhaps Linarv holds onto some of that old grief to better appreciate his life now. Something I dare not ask him directly.

"I've seen enough for today." He pushes back from the fence and gives me a nod. "You've done well with this batch."

"We all have."

"Still, your skills have improved, little star. Worthy of your family's legacy, yes?"

His words of praise make the day's work rest lighter on my shoulders. "Perhaps, but much of the credit should go to my teachers."

He claps me on the shoulder with a laugh, rich and musical, and I head toward the village. Behind me, he sings to himself:

*The Truthteller told me no lies,*
*But I ignored their pleas.*
*The Truthteller warned me,*
*But I did not have the wit to see.*

I hum along as I walk. I didn't notice how late it had gotten while Linarv and I worked. The days are growing shorter, and so does our remaining time in Astrava. I hurry toward the elders' pavilion, knowing the liaison will still be awake even if it appears motionless. Inside, the elders' voices are raised in argument, but I cannot make out the words. I wonder if the liaison can. No smoke, so it's not an official meeting. But I cannot remember a time when such serious conversations happened outside of full council sessions. Strange.

I focus my attention on the liaison, but it has no news for me. *I won't be like the others, though,* Kikriva told me once. I push back the disappointment I've grudgingly grown used to and turn back for home.

Mother's waiting for me. "What kept you so?"

"I stopped by the elders' pavilion."

"And you spoke with the liaison again." Her voice is evenly measured, but her disappointment is a tangible thing in the air between us.

"Yes. Kikriva said she'd send me word once she and her family are settled." Despite there being 168 days since they left Astrava.

"Thurava, I know it's painful, but you must resign yourself to the fact Kikriva's gone. The sooner you can accept that . . . "

"She's still my friend. I won't doubt that, no matter what you say."

Mother sighs at the look on my face. "I only speak the truth, little one. You must decide what to do with it. We leave for the graze in three days. Use that time to mourn what you've lost. To contemplate what's to come. You know we cannot afford any distractions out there."

I'm not sure what tells the lucerva it's time to leave Astrava.

The yeanlings are prone to mischief, perhaps feeding on the restless energy of the others as they prowl along their confines. Mother fusses as Linarv and Rakravat distribute our supplies in bundles along the backs of the stoutest males. As I've done for the last week, I'm tasked with teaching the yeanlings how to heed the staff of a lucerva herder. It's the only time I'm allowed to handle Mother's, made from honey-brown aged wood blended seamlessly with lucerva thigh bone.

When I tap it along the ground in a steady pattern, the lucerva must walk. When it stills, so must they. While our staffs can do much more when we are on the graze, their primary purpose is to control herd movement in coordination with whistled commands. There's also the occasional tap on rump or side to keep them on task. The animals must not fear the staff but be mindful of what it signifies. A delicate balance.

I chase them around the yeanling pen, staff tapping. Sometimes slow and steady, others a rat-a-tat trot.

Laughter cuts through the crisp morning air. A group of village boys lounge against the outermost fence. They must also sense our remaining time in Astrava runs short. Rakravat chases them away with a story of the Laborer's duty.

I shake my head as they go. "They act like what we do is so remarkable when it's just a lot of work."

"Don't be so hard on them. They don't know what it's really like to care for the herd—they only have our stories and the esteem that's been placed in the lucerva for generations."

After the Great Scatter, our people learned to tame the lucerva, and our mastery over the animals is what's allowed the Astrava to settle in this river valley, wanting for nothing. Indeed, it does seem magical the lucerva came to us at the time we needed them the most so long ago.

"If all you knew of lucerva came from the histories, how would that change you?" Rakravat asks me.

"They're still very foolish," I grumble.

He chuckles and pats my shoulder. "Most people are." He grows serious. "But that's not really an option for Sitarva of Astrava's daughter, is it?"

No. I've known my whole life I'd take my mother's place as Astrava's lucerva herder. A responsibility that's crowded out most childish impulses. I cannot afford them.

One of the yeanlings scampers up and burrows its face against me, bleating welcome. Nor would I trade this life for another. The animals, the desert, the stars—they're mine as surely as I am theirs.

The graze has a rhythm all its own, but some days it's harder to lose myself in it than others as we reacquaint the animals and ourselves to the land. We march for two nights, the stars winking overhead, and sleep in the shade of our tents during the day, trading off watching the herd in shifts. When we reach the first stretch of rangeland, we make camp and let the animals graze on grass and lichen and anything else that can make something out of the thin soil. We all relish in the quiet that comes from being away from Astrava.

The silence finally breaks when Linarv sings after supper's put away one night, his voice blending in with the flutter of the desert breeze through the darkness. A song of welcome and longing as the Joyful One's reunited with a dear friend despite the monsters that roam the land. Afterwards, Rakravat tells stories that make Mother's rich laugh roll through the herd, hundreds of fuzzy ears flicking in our direction. Even with Kikriva gone, this moment's just about perfect.

But the desert grows miserly as we travel.

"The herd will exhaust the area in but a few days," Rakravat reports two weeks later.

"So soon," Mother says softly.

I keep my attention on the fire as I rake the embers to tidy up after breakfast. I catch Rakravat's grim nod out of the corner of my eye. I cannot see Mother's face, but I can imagine her disappointment after our herd exhausted two other watering holes that have always run full in years past. We only reached this small valley yesterday, wind-sheltered with good drainage to the south. Last year, we stayed for weeks, watching the Joyful One in its travels across the sky. But Rakravat's right. The vitav's thin on the ground, when the creepers used to cushion every footfall.

"We'll stay as long as we can. Plus two days beyond that," Mother says resolutely.

"We've faced lean times before," Rakravat replies.

"And the herd will need the practice."

When Mother spots me, her face wavers with some emotion, then smooths into the confident veneer I know so well. "Before you spell Linarv, go collect vitav. I saw some plants south of camp."

Even though it feels like wasted effort, I do as I'm told. The ones I find grow along the washes, precariously perched to catch runoff from the occasional flash flood. Every plant's shallow-rooted instead of reaching deep down to where groundwater flows.

The midday sun shines down by the time I trudge back to camp, my collecting bag barely halfway full with the spiraling tendrils.

Linarv's sudden shout bounces off rock from his perch overlooking the area. Mother and Rakravat stumble out of his tent, sleep-dulled but wary. He hands Mother her staff while he readies his crossbow. Mother's gaze cuts to me, and her eyes widen in alarm. "Thurava, behind you!"

I shrug the collecting bag off my shoulder and redouble my grip on my own simple staff. Sturdy though it may be, it suddenly feels small and insubstantial.

Only one thing generates such all-consuming panic. Nazoph. I find the reptilian creature glaring at me from the underbrush, but its gruesome appearance gives me pause. They're half the size of an adult lucerva, but where the lucerva are fur and bone, nazoph have sharp teeth, claws, and thick, muscular bodies that lend their surprise attacks added strength. A monster walking out of a nightmare.

"Don't move," Mother calls out. "We're almost there."

But it's too late. The nazoph lets out a deep-bellied trill and launches itself at me with the speed and power of a lucerva kick. I knock it back with my staff—barely—the knuckles on my right hand stinging from making contact with the chitinous ridges running along its spine.

The nazoph hits the ground then it's back on its feet after a rolling twist. I land a strike on its shoulder with my staff and follow up with a jab to its chin.

Bunching its body, it prepares for another attack. One of Rakravat's bolts hits its chest, and it lets out a roar. Mother strides forward. She brings her staff down on its flat skull with a sickening thump, spreading the beast's brains across the stony ground.

Linarv joins us, dusty and disheveled from his swift descent from his lookout post. "There's more of them. This way."

He leads us past the area where I was collecting vitav. The lucerva, instead of placidly grazing, mill about, nervous energy coursing through them. We follow the current to where the lucerva broadcast their discomfort in panicked, high-pitched bleats as they pace about a little depression.

Linarv points his staff down a hill rocky with scree. Spread across on the ground, their light brown coats stained red are two adults and three yeanlings—all gone thanks to nazoph. They're the only beasts capable of such careless destruction.

"I couldn't see it from my post. Only when it approached Thurava," he says.

Mother glances back to the hillock where Linarv had been keeping watch. "You couldn't have known."

It's the truth, but Linarv still flinches at the flatness of her voice.

Rakravat examines the ground and picks out a trail of blood. Mother barrels down it, but he grabs her shoulders, holding her back. "Wait, Sitarva. We must secure the rest of the herd before—"

"*No.* This was no ordinary kill. This was savagery. And it cannot go unpunished."

"You're doing this for yourself as much as the herd," he says to her in a hard voice.

Mother whirls toward him, staff clenched tightly in her hands. He's never been one to disagree with her without cause. Something unspoken passes between them, and Rakravat lets her go.

"Thurava," her voice snaps me to attention, "you'll stay here and try to calm the herd."

I shake my head. "If there are more of them, you'll need me. You'll need all of us."

Rakravat and Linarv nod in agreement.

Mother tsks but utters no more objections as we follow her down the blood trail. I wipe my palms on my cloak, nearly sick with adrenaline.

I know why Mother's so distraught and determined. We all do. I was too young to remember all the details when Father died. Mauled by nazoph during one of his shifts watching the herd. Why he chose to confront it on his own is a question to which only the stars know the answer. Though he left us that graze over twelve years ago, his passing still ripples out, affecting all of us—Mother most of all—especially whenever nazoph are involved.

"There!" Linarv points to a rocky outcropping, the dark crevices between boulders making it a perfect fortress. A juvenile nazoph, too engorged to retreat back into its den, bristles when it notices our presence.

Linarv and Rakravat take aim with their crossbows, landing bolts in the creature's sides. A pitiful wheezing cry escapes it before it slumps down, dead.

A throaty trill fills the air, and Linarv shouts in warning as another juvenile comes scurrying out of the burrow. Rakravat lands a bolt in the creature's chest, then Mother's staff is a whirl of motion as she slams the knob of lucerva bone into its stomach, then its head, a harsh cry echoing from somewhere deep inside her.

A stick snaps behind me. I turn, hoping only a curious yeanling has followed us.

Linarv pushes me aside as a fully-grown nazoph springs toward us from the brush. He gets off a bolt into the creature's soft stomach then it's on him. I jam my staff into its side and knock it away. Rakravat takes another shot with his crossbow, then Mother comes charging over, her robes making her seem like some dark wraith bent on vengeance as she brings her staff down on the wounded nazoph.

Even once the creature's dead, she slams the staff down again with a wet, snapping pop as muscle and bone punch through the nazoph's thick skin with the impact.

"Sitarva, enough." Rakravat takes her by the shoulders and gives her a shake, his worried eyes boring into her face.

She drops the staff and steps into his arms with a sob. He holds her tight, perhaps knowing better than anyone else why she's so upset. Then she pushes him away and sweeps me into her arms. She presses her forehead to mine for a fierce moment then straightens to fuss over Linarv. Besides a few rents in his shirtsleeve, a couple of scratches, he's fine.

"Thank you, Linarv. My thanks to all of you," she says in a broken voice.

Tears prick my eyes at seeing her so diminished. She takes a deep breath, clasps Rakravat and Linarv's hands, then plants her staff, mastering herself once more. "We have much to do."

Late into the day we work. We haul the carcasses for predator and prey alike to camp, saving what we can of hide and fur, meat and bone. Nothing can go to waste. What we don't need can surely be of use to Astrava. With hides curing, meat drying, and the fire burning bright with offal, Mother breaks her silence as the first stars show themselves in the sky overhead.

"Today was a hard day after a number of hard weeks. The land around us is changing, but we must walk the desert as we always do, defiant in the face of such adversity." She levers her staff to the stars winking overhead, its surface still streaked with rusty brown blood-stains, and points to the constellation for Ceaseless Storm, a formation visible only during the shortest days of the year. "We have no choice. The herd's our destiny, our responsibility, and we'll see it through. Remember the story of Ceaseless Storm inscribed in the stars."

In the age before, a warlord desperate for allies sent his son to seek help. As the son traveled, he encountered a fierce storm that blocked the road ahead. Instead of giving up and failing in his task, he stayed the course, eventually emerging from the storm thirty days and thirty nights later on the other side of the world. When he finally led their allies back to his homeland, which was another story in and of itself, he helped his father to victory.

Mother looks to each of us. "Today was a hard day, I know. But we can do this, together, no matter what the stars set before us."

I know she chose that tale to encourage us to finish out the graze despite such setbacks. But I cannot help wondering if we're in fact the father in the story, beset by enemies and desperate for aid that might never come.

## III. Ceaseless Storm

"That should be the last of them." Rakravat fastens the gate with a relieved sigh behind the last lucerva—a stubborn male always prowling the edges of the herd for the first opportunity to bolt.

As we trudge toward the settlement, Rakravat stiffens up, as though he wears another person's skin on top of his own. While it's true he and Mother must be more discreet in Astrava than when we're on the graze, it's more than that. Whenever we're home, he becomes far more reserved, as though hoping he can blend into the landscape and avoid anyone's notice.

Some of that must stem from what happened with his family when he gave up pottery to work with the lucerva. A scandal since Rakravat was the eldest child and expected to continue on in the path of his parents. They suspected his decision wasn't out of any real fondness for the animals but because of his interest in Mother, who was otherwise untouchable as a widow. Everyone knew she'd taken Linarv on as charity years before, but Rakravat would be different. She'd never abdicate her responsibility to the herd, so he made his choice to join her the only way he could.

The rumors became so ugly, they were eventually brought before the council to answer for them. Mother argued for an exception to be made, but Janeeva and others on the council made that impossible when the price for doing so would have demoted Linarv from his position to make way for Rakravat. His family would settle for nothing but the honor of having him be the lucerva herder's second if he would not be theirs alone. Mother refused, of course, so now they must pretend they're nothing to each other when they're in Astrava to keep the peace.

Rakravat never talks about it, holding his silence in the wake of all the vicious stories that have sprung up since. Even though it all occurred when I was too young to realize what was happening, I swiftly learned to ignore the biting comments and questions intended to bait me into a response that would surely take wing through the community. After all, there's no reason for shame for my part. I'm grateful I've had Linarv and Rakravat to stand in my father's place for so long. Without them, I'd surely feel the sting of his absence more sharply. There's no question they've both helped Mother and the herd thrive.

Even though *all* of our efforts have fallen short this year.

The feast preparations drift toward us, the smoke scenting the air. Rakravat doesn't need to say we have nothing to be festive about. A handful of yeanlings died on the graze as lean days grew long, though it must be said the rest are as hale and hearty as any lucerva I've seen. Nazoph attacks were also far more frequent this year, worrying the herd's numbers and whittling them down. And yet we walked the desert as we always do.

We join Mother and Linarv. She searches the faces of those who greet us, a brittle smile on her face. So many others have left while we were away. Bravlat's family brings us an ewer of water to refresh ourselves as everyone else watches on, impatient to hear our news and unwilling to give us our customary welcome.

Without preamble, we're ushered to the fire, and the meal begins. Conversation's more subdued than in years past as people listen closely to Mother's report on the graze. "Bad luck, I know," she says after recounting our travels, "but next year will be better. May the stars make it so."

The most high merely nods at that while the others exchange concerned looks.

"What's happened?" Mother finally asks as the last platters make their way around the fire.

The most high frowns. "The harvest wasn't as plentiful as we hoped."

"Much of the grain was full of rot or stunted in growth," another elder explains.

Mother's gaze meets Linarv's across the fire. "We could harvest another male early—"

"More ground bone to fertilize the soil won't help," the most high says. "We've already tried. The Karnez have faced similar troubles. They've cut off trade, and we've seen their clans pass through Astrava on their way to the Glass City."

Mother shakes her head. "No wonder so many have left."

"Six more families in the time you were gone. Those of us who remain are understandably concerned." He lets that hang in the air. "But we've had lean years before," he finishes bracingly.

Exhaustion weighs heavily on me, but a warning hums underneath my skin at the tension in Mother's frame as her gaze flicks toward the elders' pavilion and the spindly form of the Glass City liaison stationed beside the opening. After a strained meal, I excuse myself and hurry toward it. The liaison's smooth oval face flickers at my approach.

"Has there been word from Kikriva and her family?" I ask it breathlessly. Surely it's been time enough for them to get settled.

The liaison pauses, listening intently to my words, then, ticking like a clock, it spreads its articulated metal arms wide. "There is no message, but rest assured, they are being well taken care of in Miravat."

"Are you certain?"

The response comes more quickly this time. "I am." The liaison pauses again, and something whirrs underneath its chest plate. "They were admitted to Miravat 387 days ago and are still accounted for."

I suck a breath. So long. I still miss Kikriva terribly even though I'm furious at her for forgetting her promise. When there'd been no word before we left for the graze, I hoped it was taking them longer than expected to get settled. But after so long with no message, it hurts to realize she's no different from the others who've left Astrava behind.

"We can reunite you with your friend, should you wish it."

For a moment, temptation floods me, yearning overpowering sense. And loyalty. But the only way to see Kikriva is to go to the Glass City, turning my back on Astrava, on my mother, and everything my mother's family built. How could I consider such a path, even for a moment?

The elders approach, my mother among them. She eyes my proximity to the liaison but says nothing as I reluctantly step off the pavilion to let the elders pass. Mother stays behind, a new wrinkle in her brow that wasn't there when we first returned to the settlement. She tucks my hair back from my face. "Get some rest, little one."

I bristle at the diminutive. I'm not so little. In but a few years, I'll be the one leading the herd. "But so many have left for the city."

"If that's their desire, we cannot stop them," she says in a tired voice.

"What happens when we're the only ones left?"

"Our people are resilient. If we survived the Great Scatter, we can face anything. Don't worry."

But I do anyway.

Lucerva horns bleat not welcome nor celebration but a call to gather the next day.

People leave their work and assemble in front of the elder's pavilion where the most high waits. I come from the lucerva pens and search for Mother in the crowd. She stands near the front of the gathering, exhaustion rimming her dark brown eyes, frustration tightening her mouth. She stayed late at the elders' pavilion yesterday while I slept.

The most high raises his hands, and quiet spreads through the crowd like the wind. "We face a choice, one it's our destiny to meet. You all know the difficulties we've had these past years. Drought, disruptions in trade, and the lucerva growing leaner and less numerous with every season. And you know what we risk if we continue on despite the warnings. Our friends, our families. The Glass City will open its arms, give us a place to live, a new purpose. But that means saying goodbye to Astrava, our way of life."

Murmurs ripple through the crowd. Mother stares straight ahead, tight-lipped. None of the other elders look pleased by the situation, even Janeeva, but I suspect this time they'll all abide by whatever the settlement decides. There are too few of us now to entertain the petty differences of the past.

The most high gestures to the liaison, standing at attention. "We will provide sanctuary to all," its voice rings out, fighting through layers of gears and metal plates. "We realize how difficult this decision is, and we will do all we can to make resettlement as painless as possible."

The most high clears his throat. "We'll consult the stars. At the dawning of the evening in three days' time, you must decide your fate."

Despite all the questions I've cast into the sky, the stars have never answered me directly. As the settlement gathers together—the night unfolding around us—surely that must change. But as the most high leads the inquiry, they shine down like they always do: silent, watchful, and well out of reach.

Everyone adds something to the communal pyre in the hopes the blaze will match the intensity of the stars. Perhaps that will catch their notice and guide our actions. One family places a roughspun swaddling blanket into the fire. Another a worn hide belt. Mother feeds the blaze a bone carving I don't remember seeing amongst our belongings. Maybe it was Father's or something from her childhood. And now it's gone.

Once the most high's satisfied with the fire's strength, he calls for the marking stones and sets them along the base of the pyre. "The stones will show us the path ahead based on which constellations still glimmer as the fire dies. We must all bear witness."

The stones soon burn red-hot, the constellations they depict shining brilliant white. I watch the blaze until my eyes water, waiting along with everyone else for the stars to speak to us.

It takes hours. Feet aching, eyes bleary, I scarcely believe it when the fire burns low. A strong gust of wind from the west gutters the flames. Everyone assembled holds their breath as we wait to see which stones stay lit the longest.

But they go dark so quickly after one another, no one can say which constellation shone the longest. Undeterred, the most high instructs us to assemble the next evening and place the same questions before the stars.

This time, one stone bursts from the fire in blazing pieces, followed by two more. The concussive pops echo in my chest.

A flash of dismay passes over the most high's face or maybe it's just a trick of the light and my tired eyes. He raises his hands for calm. "There's no need for alarm. The stones overheated."

A group of elders speak with the most high in hushed voices while the rest of us watch on uneasily. Janeeva hisses, "We cannot keep this up, Torvat."

The most high doesn't acknowledge her or the others. "In darkness our people made a creature so complete, all our needs it would meet." He starts to sing, his voice thready at first, then strengthens with the epic tale of how the lucerva were created in Eternity's Stomach.

*When darkness ruled the land*
*And scattered our people far and wide*
*The Laborer faced the stars and*
*Begged for a helper to work alongside.*

*In Eternity's Stomach, lucerva were born*
*And sent to Astrava, their new home.*
*Milk, meat, bone, hide*
*Fur, hoof, horn provide*

*What the lucerva grant, the Astrava pay back.*
*The stars' blessing, our hallowed compact.*
*Milk, meat, bone, hide*
*Fur, hoof, horn provide*

Tears slide down my cheeks, Mother's too. Even stolid Rakravat swipes at his eyes. The most high's hoarse voice scrapes as we're dismissed for a final period of reflection.

More like mourning, for we all know there are no good choices here. Like Serpent's Fork hanging over the Glass City every evening.

"How can we know our fate if the stars won't talk to us?" I ask Mother as we walk back to our pavilion.

"They talk to us all the time. *We're* the ones who've forgotten how to listen. Once, scholars had special tools to capture starlight and divine their secrets. Now . . . " She sighs.

It's hard to believe our people have done so much to only fall so far. "But the most high—"

"He preserves the ceremony. Such a decision shouldn't be made lightly. Consulting the stars reminds us all of our responsibility to Astrava and to each other."

"If this is all for show . . . "

"Sometimes that's all we have."

"But—"

"Thurava." Mother's rough voice silences the rest of my question. "The stars are lost to us, just as so many of our people's achievements before the Great Scatter. Knowledge and expertise gone before either of us were born. That's our truth. That history is what we pay respect to every time we lift our faces to the stars."

"But that won't matter if we go to the Glass City."

"A different philosophy guides their people, that much is true. Even if we're to live among them, we don't have to forget where we came from."

"So you've decided, then." Once, such a proposal would have infuriated her. Where has that woman gone?

Mother's mouth firms, distaste and determination both. "I'll abide by the settlement's decision. As will you."

The next day, the people of Astrava go about their work half-heartedly, speaking in whispers and low voices if they speak at all. When the most high calls another gathering, there are no clouds, normally a good omen. But that only seems to highlight the seriousness of the occasion. "I've spoken with all of you these past few days, and we're in accord. We will entrust our futures to the Glass City."

The lack of surprise amongst all gathered hurts in a way I've never experienced before. Was our situation so hopeless? Or did our lack of hope make it so?

"We'll begin packing tomorrow," the most high announces.

The liaison clicks and whirrs and raises its spindly arms. "That will not be necessary. We will be on hand to assist you in the morning. I have already informed my counterparts of your decision."

There's no feast, no songs, no words of comfort as we return to our pavilions. Mother and I pack up our things in silence, the actions routine after so many times doing the same thing on the eve of the graze. When I lay down on my sleeping platform for the last time, Mother kneels beside me and kisses my forehead like I'm a little girl.

Then she leaves our pavilion. No doubt to be with Rakravat. That she's no longer trying to hide it means Astrava must truly be gone.

The truth of the liaison's words greets us the next morning. Dozens of nearly identical machines, gleaming in the sun, have arrived to help us gather up our lives and place them on the motorized caravan they've brought along.

In accounts of the age before, I learned of war machines on huge rollers like the caravan waiting for us on the northern edge of the settlement. It's hard to look at it and not marvel at its scale, the construction necessary to make it functional.

As we move through the settlement to meet up with Rakravat and Linarv who should already be at the lucerva pens, we come across Bravlat, the toolmaker, arguing with one of the liaisons. "What do you mean I cannot bring my livelihood?" he exclaims.

The liaison holds up its hands, mimicking entreaty. "We will be able to recreate anything you need. There is no need to bring any of this to Miravat."

Bravlat stands defensively over a crate of tools made of bone and stone, a few glinting with precious metal, handles wrapped in supple lucerva hide. "What about personal belongings?"

The liaison nods. "They will need to pass inspection, but that is a small matter."

Mother rests her hand on my shoulder. "Come, we must see to the lucerva." Reluctantly, we leave Bravlat to his packing.

A liaison follows us, a slight judder to its stride over the uneven terrain. "You are wasting time."

Mother whirls around, and it comes to a clumsy stop. "What do you mean?"

"The beasts cannot come to Miravat. It is forbidden."

For a moment, I think Mother will strike the liaison with her staff, so dark the look in her eyes. But she merely tightens her grip and stalks toward the most high where he stands besieged by questions near the central cookfire. "We weren't given all the information when we made our decision, Torvat," Mother says, voice clipped but furious. That she uses his given name and not his title draws everyone's attention toward us better than the blast of a lucerva horn. "They say we must leave the herd behind."

"Sitarva, please." The most high's gaze begs her for calm. "We'll work out a compromise."

She plants her staff. "If we don't bring the herd, they'll die."

The liaison crosses its spindly arms over its body in something like disapproval. "The beasts cannot come. We have sources of protein comparable to what the lucerva provide you, and we manufacture a wide variety of fabrics that are superior to the hides you rely on to clothe your people."

Those aren't the only things the lucerva provide us, but it's telling what the Glass City liaisons are focused on—tangible products a machine can measure, not symbolism that lives and breathes.

"They cannot be left here. I won't allow it." Mother shakes her head. "The lucerva have nurtured the people of Astrava for generations. We cannot turn our backs on them."

The most high hisses and grips Mother's elbow. "Think about what you're saying, Sitarva."

She shakes him off her. "You cannot be the same man who sang of the lucerva's founding with such feeling."

"It's a way to recognize all they've done for us, but—"

She stares at him, aghast. "I cannot believe you'd have us abandon them." Her gaze falls to me, and her face wavers into resolve. "No. If there's no place for the herd in the Glass City, then there's no place for me."

"Agreed." Rakravat steps forward, catches Mother's eye, and gives her a firm nod.

Linarv joins them. "I'll stay as well."

Mother turns to me, her voice strong when she says, "Thurava, you'll go to the city and seek your fortune."

I've trained to be a lucerva herder my whole life. To go to Miravat without the animals or my mother beside me? Unthinkable. "How can you tell me that?" How can she decide *my* future in the space of a breath?

She closes her eyes as if pained. "You have a chance to break the pattern. To see what else the stars hold for you." She steps closer and cups my cheeks.

My hands cover hers, but I'm not sure if it's to draw her closer or fling her away from me. "But the lucerva. They would be my responsibility too." In a few years, *I'll* be the one leading the herd, taking over for my mother as she did for hers the time before.

"No longer," Mother says firmly. "I couldn't choose this if it meant taking you on a path with no future."

I pull out of her grip. "But what of *your* future?" She has to know the desert cannot support them forever if what the elders say is true.

"My fate's tied to the herd, whatever comes. You'll start anew, be reborn in the Glass City." Her face hardens. "I wouldn't demand it of you if I wasn't certain you could succeed, Thurava. You're my daughter, capable of anything. May you always shine brightly."

But alone? Without the last of my family? I doubt anyone can be that strong.

Mother mistakes my silence for agreement and presses a marking stone into my hand, still ashy from the pyre the night before. My fingertips trace the constellation for the Great Navigator. "Like so many stars before us, you have a chance to go on the best you can. Take it."

## IV. Serpent's Fork

Linarv and Rakravat meet me before I board the strange motorized caravan belching smoke and smelling of sulfur. Mother, the most high, and the other elders argue while liaisons help people load their belongings into compartments along the vehicle's flanks. Despite all the activity, the buzz of anticipation and anxiety, I'm lost in myself.

I'm being cast out of Astrava. By my own mother. Not even the coldest day of the year can cut me so.

Linarv's thick fingers brush the tears from my cheek.

Rakravat gives me a sad smile. "Sitarva only wants what's best for you," he tells me.

"It doesn't feel that way."

"Your mother's sending you away to keep our stories alive. It's an honor that wounds, true, but it's an honor no less." He watches me closely. "If not that, then think of the other children who are going. They don't have your strength and will need your guidance."

I can only nod miserably. So swiftly my future's been recast as a leader of children, not lucerva. A demotion in my eyes if not theirs.

Behind me, a baby cries, unconvinced by the soothing noises their mother makes as they board the caravan. At least they get to be together in Miravat.

"Kikriva will be glad to see you, I'm certain," Linarv adds. That's something, though it comes twisted around her broken promise to me like a thorny creeper strangling a flower. "The stars' path for us isn't always clear, Thurava."

I shake my head. "Looking for patterns where there are none will turn you cross-eyed."

They both chuckle, then Linarv speaks. "We just wanted you to remember you'll have friends there, even if you won't have us."

Linarv and Rakravat. Mother. Me. After Father died, the four of us made a new life together, even if that wasn't the stars' intention for us at first. Now, I can see it no other way even as I'm expected to start over again once more. This time alone.

Linarv pulls a walking staff from behind his back, nearly as beautiful as Mother's, intricate with carvings and topped with a knob of polished bone. "Rakravat helped me make it. We were saving it for . . . " When I take over the herd. Linarv shakes his head. "This way you'll have something worthy of you in the Glass City."

My numbness thaws as he pushes the staff into my hands. The smooth wood, painstakingly sanded down to match the bone, is warm to the touch. I fight the sob in my throat. "My thanks to you both."

"It's a little long," Rakravat says with a critical eye at the line of my shoulders compared to the staff's height, "but you'll grow into it." He sounds so certain. If only I could be as well.

Horns sound, and liaisons usher the remaining stragglers toward the caravan. A fresh wave of tears escapes my eyes.

"Never forget, Thurava, daughter of Sitarva," Linarv rumbles in his deep, musical voice, "you are the star of Astrava."

Both of them clasp my hands in turn, then Mother's here—fierce and beautiful and *home* all at once—as she bundles me into her arms. Any anger at being sent away is quenched by a sense of loss so great I can only glimpse the edges of it as I clutch her to me. "May the stars shine down on you, daughter."

Then she puts my reluctant hand into that of the most high. She holds his gaze for a long moment, broken only by his bow to her. A formal goodbye, expansively given, to a superior. Mother remains unswayed by the gesture. The most high purses his mouth as we turn toward the caravan. If he wasn't here to coax me on board like a timid yeanling, I'm not certain I'd be able to do it myself. He leads me to a bench with a tall back near a window looking out on what's left of Astrava.

The terraced bluffs are scrubbed clean of any evidence of our people, interrupted only by skeletal pavilions and empty workstalls. The lucerva graze in the distance, too far for any distinguishing characteristics aside from their brown and tan coats. Perhaps it's better this way. A general impression devoid of specifics to carry with me.

Mother once said she wished she could forget Father, envious of my child's memory that could barely piece together an image of his face, let alone anything more solid. Memories can cut as well as any weapon.

I didn't believe her until today. The Truthteller, always. I should know by now to heed it. And yet to be sent away . . .

The caravan fills with my fellow Astravans, all of them ready to face the future the Glass City's offered us. While some tremble with excitement, others share in my grief and uncertainty, their faces pinched with repressed emotion, eyes red from tears or the threat of them. Soon, every seat's full. Only my family remains beyond the transport's windowpanes.

Afternoon tumbles into twilight, but Mother stands firm, Linarv and Rakravat at her side, as the caravan shudders into motion. I don't know how she could simply watch while Astrava was dismantled around her. How she could let us pack up and leave as though it's any other day. But she's doing it for the herd. In my heart, I know this, no matter how much it hurts.

She must stay behind if others in Astrava will not. Just as her mother's mother made the difficult decision to stop raising lucerva for their milk when the Najimov couldn't keep both their grazing lands and that of the settlement's grain watered. A choice causing considerable upset at the time. The herd survived that and adapted. So will it again under Mother's leadership, if not mine.

May the stars make it so.

We cross the desert, roughly following the banks of the Najimov to where it disappears at the base of the Glass City's walls. As Miravat's towers grow closer, for the first time I allow myself to wonder what sort of future looms before me. Like many in Astrava, I've tried hard not to think about the city and what it represents. But despite the elders' warnings, I'm chagrined to find I've subconsciously dreamt of a life not tied to the lucerva. Such thoughts are like the grubs found in the seedpods of our grain. You don't know they're there until you have cause to split them open. Only then is the extent of the rot known.

No wonder we were taught to avert our eyes for so long.

Serpent's Fork dawns and strengthens as darkness settles over our caravan. The others have turned their backs to what the constellation portends, denying with body language what they dare not say aloud.

The starlight tells the tale of a woman, heavy with child, who runs away from her family fearing shame and censure. A serpent appears and tells her one path leads to the home of a man who will give her shelter. There she'll be able to raise her child, but she'll never be able to escape the man's cruel nature. The other road takes her through dangerous and difficult terrain. She risks losing the baby, and there's no guarantee she'll be welcomed in the next city. Does she settle for what's known or put her trust in harsh uncertainty?

There are variations where the woman chooses one path over the other, resulting in different interpretations of the tale and what it means for us. The most high once said the actual choice doesn't matter so much as a person's commitment to it. But that brings little comfort as the caravan lurches and creaks through the night.

Too soon, the city's glow eclipses even my view of the stars.

No one knows what to expect when the transport finally rumbles to a stop late the next morning. The same liaisons that ushered us out of Astrava escort us into a large building set outside the massive, mirrored walls of the city. I cannot see what wonders lay beyond the glass, but I hope Kikriva's on the other side. Surely she's heard we're coming.

Along one wall, a rectangular basin pumps water out in clear, tinkling arcs. We're all given the opportunity to refresh ourselves, marveling at such an unexpected luxury. Afterwards, we're told to group ourselves together by family. That catches me like a burr. I have no family anymore. Or, rather, I'm my own family now here in this place.

An idea I still haven't gotten used to.

I drift toward the edge of the room, creeping closer to a hallway leading into the city proper. The liaisons are so busy seeing to the others, no one pays attention to me as I slip through translucent curtains, surprisingly heavy and slick to the touch. There's a table covered in stacks of books with metal covers. I nearly stop but spy the archway at the end of the hall and the sunlight streaming through it.

After being told not to look at the Glass City my whole life, being denied now is almost unbearable. Mother always said we must bear witness. Especially now, I tell myself.

The corridor opens onto a crowded street. I half-expect to see more liaisons with their awkward, metallic limbs and cold, clockwork features marching through the streets. But these are people of flesh and blood. Even if a goodly number of them wear beetle-like lenses or translucent veils to protect their eyes from the glare cast from practically every surface. Some have skin dark as night. Others are so pale, I'm surprised the sun hasn't marked them in some way. Many are golden brown like the people of Astrava, but their skin isn't coarse or toughened by the elements. I scarcely know where to look since any other similarities end there.

I've met the occasional trader from Karnez in my travels and exhausted Astrava's store of books many times over, but the disorienting parade of humanity makes me wish I spent more time talking with the liaison stationed in Astrava, no matter what Mother would have thought of it.

A small child points at me, and people begin to stare. I make a short bow of greeting.

For a moment, hushed silence is my answer. Then a man a few feet away sneezes. Others follow, and a wave of startled dismay runs through the crowd. Someone gestures to me, and heated chatter breaks out. I never made an effort to learn the Miravat language, not with the graze and the herd taking up so much of my time. I don't know what's being said, but it's certainly directed at me. A lifetime ago, Kikriva said the people here wear different clothes. Perhaps my roughspun pants and hide tunic are a strange sight to them.

But the bewildering anger in their gazes makes me take a step back. I run into something hard, metallic. A liaison looks down at me. "You should not be here. Come." Its placid expression's at odds with its voice—projected much more forcefully than I've ever heard before. Its hand clamps onto my shoulder and physically steers me back the way I came. "You must not enter the city yet."

"I only wanted to—"

"You will have every opportunity to explore *after* you are cleared for entry."

The cool metal fingers bite into my skin but lack any real force behind them. The metal creatures are unnerving with their strange appearance and elongated limbs, but they're not particularly nimble. I remember how they stumbled across the rocky soil in Astrava and have difficulty manipulating small objects with their crude hands. I'm certain I could wrench free of the liaison's grip and stay out of its reach if I truly wished it, but something coils low in my gut at the thought of going against the liaison's wishes now as I'm escorted back inside.

One by one, we're called into the next chamber. When it's my turn, I enter a white room sharp with medicinal herbs though I see no plants or tinctures anywhere. A liaison waits for me, its face jittering nonstop like a ripple across water, making it difficult to focus on its empty eyes. "In order for you to pass through the walls of the city, you must renounce everything made from lucerva components, including your clothes. Bone is the only exception."

I'll be able to keep the marking stone and staff but . . . "Why?"

"These precautions will prevent you from making the people of Miravat sick."

"Sick? Is that why those people started sneezing?" I ask, thinking of my brief glimpse of the Glass City.

The liaison clicks and whirrs, but its face gives no hint of its thoughts. "Please remove your clothing and walk through the gate. In the next room, you will be given new clothes."

I work off my boots and stand them next to one another. They saw me safely across the desert and back the last few years, the leather shiny in some places and scuffed in others. But they cannot accompany me any longer. Surprised by my nostalgia, I straighten, spreading my toes on the cool floor tiles. Forcing back revulsion at the liaison's presence, I lift my hide tunic over my head. It drops to the stone floor with a soft slap. Kikriva's family made it for me two years ago. My roughspun pants and undertunic follow, along with my hide belt.

Before I give into the urge to cover myself, I approach the gate. It seems to sense my presence and lights up. Rays as bright as the sun's bathe my body as I pass through. On the other side, I'm given bootlets and a white tunic made of a slippery soft material. It takes a moment to understand how it's supposed to be tied shut. I smooth the fabric over my hips. Kikriva was right—it feels like wearing nothing at all.

"Thank you for your compliance," the liaison announces once I'm fully dressed. "Now please join the others."

We gather in the hall as we wait for everyone to pass through the light gate and don their borrowed clothes. Some of the younger children dart about, chasing each other. No wonder after being trapped on the transport so long. The adults speak in small groups, someone occasionally reaching out to admire the drape of the new clothes or to point out a feature of our surroundings. The walls, the fountain, the liaisons where they motionlessly stand watch.

One of them addresses us once we're all assembled. "You will have the opportunity to collect your personal belongings in a moment. But first, know, regardless of what path you choose to take in our city, you will always be welcome at the Astrava lodge, where you can live until you get your bearings in Miravat. You will also be given a device to help you navigate the city since many of you are not familiar with our language and customs. We believe everyone has a use, and we look forward to finding out the best way you can contribute to our society."

We're dismissed to gather our personal items. I'm relieved to have my staff in hand and the marking stone in a pocket close to my heart. Then I'm sent toward the hall to line up with the others. There, we're given one of the metal books I saw earlier. No. Now that I hold one in my hands, I realize it's not a book. No pages, just a glassy top cover and a metallic casing similar to the material the liaisons are built from. A chain allows it to hang from our necks.

"This is a reckoner. Speak your questions into it. It will aid your exploration of Miravat. It is also your legal advocate and will help you enter into agreements with others in the city." The liaison cocks its head. "Do you understand?"

I nod.

"Then place your palm on the screen." The glassy surface shimmers with light underneath my hand, and a strange heat pulses through me. "Please state your name so the reckoner can speak to you."

"Thurava, daughter of Sitarva."

"Welcome to Miravat, Thurava, daughter of Sitarva." I try not to jump at the tinny voice drifting up from the device.

The liaison gestures to the person behind me, and I step forward with the reckoner's light still sparking in my eyes. When I enter the city this time, the crowds barely protest my arrival and that of the others from Astrava. They sift about us like water around boulders, eager to be on their way. Some wrap scarves around their faces or avert their gaze, but at least no angry voices greet me. I soon lose track of the other Astravans as we're pulled in different directions by the crowds. In the absence of familiar faces, my heartbeat quickens.

"What can I help you with, Thurava, daughter of Sitarva?"

I realize my hands are tightly clenched around the device. "Take me to Kikriva," I say despite the growing resentment she wasn't here to welcome me to the Glass City.

The screen flashes, then an arrow appears. "Follow me."

And in poor imitation of the Great Navigator consulting a map of the stars, I do.

I have to shade my eyes to properly make out the towering stone buildings that line Miravat's streets. The polished surfaces glimmer in the midday sun, some of the rock pale with veins of crystal, others dark with flecks of mica.

Cramped shops along the street give way to living quarters on the many floors above. Smoke, sewage, and an array of cooking smells scent the air along with perfume and incense to cover up the stench of so many bodies. Occasional trees provide shade. Fountains splash softly at intersections. The Najimov itself cuts through the city's eastern edge, with footbridges connecting streets and the buildings on either side. People with baskets full of trade goods stalk the crowds, shouting in Miravat. The Glass City has more citizens than I ever imagined, each with a sense of purpose to their confident strides that eludes me. I've always been sure-footed and certain in my path. But that was before I came here.

Perhaps, once I find Kikriva, I'll feel better.

In the age before, cities such as this were commonplace, with commerce and trade, arts and manufacturing, anything and everything to keep their inhabitants in comfort and wealth. Before their technologies soured and spoiled the land for generations. Before the Great Scatter fractured communities and alliances.

That Miravat might rival all the cities that came before is truly astonishing.

As I walk, the reckoner asks me questions. About my family, about my experience with the lucerva, about my goals for my stay in the Glass City. I feel foolish, speaking to it like it's a ghost trapped in a book, but I slowly get used to the device. It's too useful not to.

"Thurava, daughter of Sitarva, have you thought about where you will live in the city?"

The liaison said all Astravans could stay at the lodge until they are established. But after that? "Somewhere I can see the stars at night. And you can simply call me Thurava."

The reckoner's silent for a moment. "Understood, Thurava. Stars are only visible along the outermost edge of the upper city. There are no vacancies you can afford at the moment."

"Afford? What do you mean?"

"Every citizen is given a certain allotment to live on each quarter—roughly the equivalent to Astrava's seasons. That is not sufficient for an apartment in the upper city. You will need to acquire a trade to supplement your income. Based on your age and experience, I can provide you with suggestions."

"No. Right now, I only want to see my friend."

The reckoner takes me towards the center of the city, leaving the bustle of the lower section with its market stalls and busy storefronts behind. My calves begin to ache. The twisting side streets have a subtle incline—something I would have noticed sooner if I wasn't surrounded by buildings that block my line of sight. Wide-open desert, though at times lonely, never lied to my senses the way the Glass City does now.

The reckoner leads me to a large building. Unlike the ones in the lower city, it's not carved up into different shops. A finely wrought gate depicting the Rask Mountains to the northwest leads to a private courtyard full of lush, leafy plants and the musical tinkle of water.

"I have alerted the household of your arrival," the reckoner tells me.

My heart jitters even as my eyes dart about, hoping to take in all the details of the oasis I've found myself in. Even the rainiest years in Astrava never produced such greenery. I breathe in the musty sweet scent of the delicate yellow flowers that erupt from one of the bushes like miniature suns. The door whooshes open on hidden rollers, and I start like a guilty yeanling who's wandered too far away from the herd.

Kikriva looks at me, eyes wide with disbelief. "Thurava, is it really you?"

My chest squeezes at the sight of my old friend. She's grown taller in our time apart, but that's not the only change. Her face has thinned out, chin and cheekbones as though cut from rock. Her hair, always a mischievous tumble, is separated into two smooth brown plaits. I have to squint to see the girl I knew.

Happy relief quickly gives way to the anger and disappointment I've tried so long to keep buried. Unsure what to say, I fall back on formality. "What you know of Astrava is no more. I've come to seek a new life here as you have." I hold out my hands. "You look well."

Kikriva blushes and for a moment clasps my hands in return so hard I nearly gasp. "I didn't expect—" She shakes her head. "You shouldn't be here. I—"

"Why not?"

She makes a gesture toward my simple clothes and the reckoner attached to the chain around my neck. "My patron—"

She whirls around as a Miravat citizen comes forward from the depths of the house as though our words conjured her into being. They have a quick exchange I cannot follow. The reckoner's screen flashes, and a moment later a translation of the rolling, musical words of the Miravat language scrolls across it.

"Who's this?" Kikriva's patron asks.

"A friend from my old life," Kikriva responds.

Her patron's an elderly woman arrayed in a beautiful tunic. Metal threads infuse the fabric and sparkle with each breath. Her bold, beady gaze quickly sweeps over me. "How nice. Did she just arrive?"

Before I can answer, Kikriva nods hastily. "Yes. She doesn't know the city's customs. She means no offense coming here like this."

"Of course." The woman's gaze lands on my reckoner and narrows. "Take the afternoon to see to her needs. Hopefully the neighbors haven't noticed her yet."

"You're most kind."

The woman waves her hand as if batting away an insect. "Be back for dinner service."

Kikriva lowers her head. "I will."

The woman sweeps back inside, and the door slides shut. Kikriva looks at it, blinking rapidly for a long moment, then turns to me. We might have been parted for a long time, but I still recognize my friend's false smile. "What's wrong?" I ask.

Kikriva doesn't answer. Instead, she loops her arm in mine and leads me back down to the lower city.

"When you left no message with the liaisons, I feared—" I force back the old pain. "I'm glad to see you well."

Her steps slow. "I *did* send messages. You're the one who didn't reply to me."

The hurt in her voice sounds real enough, but I don't dare trust my heart in this matter. "Are you saying the liaison in Astrava lied to me?"

She lets out a heavy breath. "I don't know. The liaisons may keep Miravat running, but they're far from perfect." She shakes her head. "Something must have happened." She turns to me. "I'm sorry you thought I forgot about you."

"If it's as you say, there's nothing to be sorry for."

With that we find ourselves back on fragile footing, leaving old hurts in the past and wondering at the people we've become in our time apart. She squeezes my hand, and we continue on, arms linked.

"How's the rest of your family?" I ask.

"Mother's found work as a seamstress, and Father works at a factory that makes clothes."

Factory. I supposed I shouldn't be surprised the Glass City has those as well. They appear to have everything else that's gone missing since the Great Scatter.

"And your brother?"

"He's in school. I was too, but then Devanettu offered to be my patron."

"What does that mean?"

Kikriva's brow wrinkles as we pass through a large crowd that's popped up at the intersection of two streets. "I help see to the needs of her household. In exchange, she pays for my food and clothing.

I also get a wage so I can help my parents move into the upper city one day."

"I thought you came here to do what you couldn't do in Astrava."

At the sudden dark look on Kikriva's face, I wish I hadn't spoken. But what's already been said hangs between us nonetheless.

"You don't understand anything about Miravat or you wouldn't have embarrassed me today." Kikriva takes a deep breath, and her anger disappears. "I'm glad you are here, Thurava, but you cannot visit me at Devanettu's home so boldly as you did today. At least not until you learn the customs." She glances at the people milling about the square and frowns. My shoulders stiffen at the idea she could be ashamed at being seen with me. She grits her teeth and leans toward me. "Stay in the Astrava lodge and *learn*," she whispers in my ear. "I visit my parents in the factory district on the first of each month. I'll meet you there."

"But—"

The pained look on her face silences my protests.

"It's only a few days," she says briskly.

So long. She has her own life here now, as I well know, but for a moment, it feels like she's leaving me all over again.

"Tell the reckoner, and it'll remind you." At that, I realize she has no reckoner of her own. Given the time she's been here, perhaps she has no need of one anymore. Or she's grown better at hiding it. With one last squeeze of my hand, Kikriva vanishes back the way we came. Not once does she look back. I cannot help but think she's eager to be rid of me.

I face the reckoner. "What did I do wrong?"

"You are in accordance with the city's laws."

"But she was embarrassed by me."

No response. I give the device a shake. My neck tingles, and I realize the current of people crossing the square has slowed to a trickle as it passes by me. Some point at my clothes and hair. Others whisper behind their hands. Anxiety lurches about in my chest, trying to claw its way out my throat.

"Take me to the Astrava lodge."

The reckoner flashes. "As you wish."

Night's fallen by the time I reach the lodge, a large building set along the outermost wall of the city. I couldn't have found a point further from the upper city if I tried. My eyes still ache from all the reflected light, but the long walk helped settle my mind after the day's events. I'm even able to greet the Astravans gathered in the common room with a smile as their conversations quiet for a few seconds at my entrance. By now, everyone must realize my mother charged me with coming here. Our family's always been the source of much speculation over the years, but this is the first time I must weather it alone.

Rakravat's aunt Janeeva pointedly looks away. If I were feeling more kindly, I'd feel sorry for her ever thinking Rakravat would choose the Glass City over Mother.

The chatter resumes, and Bravlat approaches. His welcoming smile crinkles the corners of his tired eyes. My own exhaustion unfurls through me, not all of it from our travels. "Thurava, you're in room 407." He hands me a simple metal key. "Please know you can count on my family if you need anything. Your mother would—" He cuts that thought off at the raw pain flickering across my face.

"Thank you," I say sincerely.

Though free of the hostile glances I encountered on Miravat's streets, I have no appetite to remain here and make small talk with my fellow Astravans. While we've all lost something in coming to the Glass City, I can no longer pretend I haven't been wounded by what happened. I envy the others for being able to still smile and laugh like we're on the eve of some grand adventure.

I find the stairs and climb them to the fourth floor. The Great Navigator surely stayed in such buildings like this in their travels. I wish stories of their exploits had better prepared me for this moment. I clasp the marking stone to my heart for a fierce moment then let it go to unlock the door to my room.

It's a tiny space, barely large enough for a bed and wardrobe and window, tucked tightly against the eaves of the roof. Chilly without my cloak. I wrap the worn but clean blanket left on the bed around my shoulders, and I look out the window despite what I won't be able to see. But just knowing the stars are overhead—*somewhere*—is enough for me to eventually find sleep in my strange new home.

"I have compiled a list of occupations you would be suited for, Thurava," the reckoner greets me the next morning. "Would you like to see?"

I blearily stare down at the screen hanging from my neck. The morning sun streams in unchecked through my window. At least I was able to sleep last night, if not well.

The reckoner blinks up at me, waiting for my response. "Not yet. I think we better start with the city first."

In Astrava, the liaisons made it seem like it'd be simple enough for us to come to the Glass City, but my conversation with Kikriva yesterday certainly showed otherwise. I should have realized sooner the folly of trusting a machine on such an important matter. We all should have.

"I want to know the customs here." I may not have done anything officially wrong in seeking Kikriva out yesterday, but clearly I misunderstood something fundamental about the way things work here. "Particularly the upper city."

The reckoner flashes. "Upper city residents are comprised primarily of Miravat's founding families and foreigners who have grown wealthy through trade and manufacturing. Such status announces itself in ways that may be invisible to outsiders." The upper city was certainly cleaner and less populated than other districts. "Clothing can often signal importance as well."

Devanettu's shimmery tunic comes to mind. "And what do the clothes given to us when we arrived signify?"

The reckoner flashes for a moment, like a heartbeat. "Those clothes signify you are new to the city and devoid of resources."

Like lucerva with rare white markings in a sea of brown and tan. No wonder Devanettu wanted me gone from her home, though at least she wasn't cruel about it, for Kikriva's sake if not mine.

"Still, our arrival at Devanettu's house surprised them."

"We appeared after customary visiting hours, but that was deemed of lesser import than reuniting you with your friend."

Visiting hours? What other rules govern the days here?

"If it is easier for you, Thurava, I can compile a list of common customs that you would benefit from knowing, and you will be able to consult them whenever you wish."

"Why couldn't you do this yesterday?" *Before* I embarrassed Kikriva.

The reckoner flashes, the pulses of light coming more swiftly this time. "I did not know of your interest in city customs yesterday."

I blow out a breath, but my annoyance at the device remains. "And the stares I got yesterday? Were they because I'm seen as a stranger to the city?"

"There are many aspects of human behavior I am ill-equipped to counsel you on."

"Then can you make a guess?"

The reckoner goes dark for a long moment. "Perhaps it is because some citizens are more welcoming of people new to the city than others."

The most high taught us the Impulsive One isn't inherently bad, even though their rash actions can create problems for themselves and others. To invite new experiences and be open to learning new things are moments when the Impulsive One thrives in our hearts. But it seems too many people here have closed their minds to such opportunities. I think over all the reckoner's told me. Maybe once we're better able to meet the citizens of Miravat on their own terms, relations will improve.

I still have more questions than answers, but I've learned enough to know I'll need to pick a trade soon if I'm going to do as Mother wishes and start anew. "What occupations do you think will suit me?"

The reckoner displays a short list. "Point to an entry to learn more."

I go through each item, then again to make sure I understand. "These are all Laborer positions." Many are at factories like the one Kikriva mentioned her father worked at. I haven't forgotten the way her nose wrinkled as she said it, either.

"Yes, Thurava."

"But in Astrava, I was a lucerva herder." Only the elders are held in higher esteem.

"Miravat has no need for herders." True enough. I've seen no animals besides the occasional songbird since coming to Miravat.

"But you are strong, used to being on your feet for long periods of time, and have experience in a wide variety of fine motor control activities. All skills suited to a laborer."

From an early age, Astravans are taught to respect the Laborer, always winking at us in the night sky. Never without their shovel, ever ready to lend a hand, to work with no expectation other than a job well done. An honorable path, certainly. But one that was never supposed to be mine.

The marking stone for the Great Navigator weighs down my pocket. Mother sent me here for a brighter future than even that of a lucerva herder. Laboring at some Miravat factory isn't a path I'd choose for myself, no matter the wonders they make.

"I don't want a Laborer's work. I am Thurava, daughter of Sitarva, and I would be more."

The reckoner's screen goes blank. "No patron would have you as you are."

"But Kikriva found one."

"Your friend has experience managing a household from a young age."

And I don't, going off on the graze for two seasons out of the year. Kikriva spent that time cooking, cleaning, and supporting her parents' work. I think of the Serpent's Fork overhead, hidden by all the buildings and the light they reflect day or night. "I can navigate the stars. I know the old stories. I can learn."

The reckoner flashes. I imagine it's thinking hard. "Would you work as a lorist?" it finally asks. "It requires years of study at Miravat's academy, delaying any increase in income. But when training is complete, you will be given a respected position. It is a modest life but an honorable one."

*Your mother's sending you away to keep our stories alive. It's an honor that wounds, true, but it's an honor no less.*

"That sounds acceptable."

"I will send your petition to the academy. In the meantime, you must remain at the Astrava lodge since you will be unable to afford other accommodations."

"I understand."

Feeling like I've accomplished something for the first time since my arrival, I join the others in the common room. Some are in conversation with their reckoners, others speak in low voices in groups of twos and threes. A large pot of gruel sits on a table, and I help myself to a bowl.

The most high sits in the corner, a liaison motionless at his side. He meets my gaze and beckons me over to the empty chair beside him. "How have you found the Glass City so far, Thurava?"

"It's a strange place, but I hope to make sense of it soon." I bite my lip. "What occupation have you chosen, if I may ask?"

He gives the liaison standing beside him a rueful look. It's missing the thumb on its left hand. "I've been told most elders are too old to learn a trade. So we shall stay here and live on the charity of our neighbors. After so many difficult years in Astrava, I suppose we've earned our rest." He grimaces at the surprise on my face I cannot smooth away in time. "Don't worry. What the people of Miravat view as charity will be bounty to us."

I take his empty bowl and my own and set them on a tray for washing. As I return to the most high's side, I pass Janeeva, who pushes at her food half-heartedly with her spoon.

"How could anyone eat this slop?" When no one answers, her sharp green gaze finds me. "Well?"

I shrug. "I've had much worse meals on the graze."

Her face twists into a sneer. "How could I forget. Running wild the minute you left Astrava, no doubt thanks to that mother of yours."

Her words strike to the very quick of me. I grab the back of my chair for the balance I've yet to find within the Glass City's walls. But it's not nearly enough to stop the wash of pain from being sent away from my family, my home.

The entire room goes deathly silent. Then, "Mind your tongue," Bravlat says. "It's not Thurava's fault the accommodations aren't to your liking."

Janeeva turns her scowl on him. "You forget who you're talking to, toolmaker."

Bravlat's smile is devoid of any warmth. "The elders' council died with Astrava. Without your status to wield, think carefully how many friends you actually have here, Janeeva."

She abruptly gets to her feet. Her gaze sweeps over the room. She must not like what she sees for she strides out, head held high, without another word.

Slowly—too slowly for my liking—people return to their meals or their conversations that were interrupted. Bravlat catches my eye and gives me a nod. I can only nod back, still troubled by what happened.

I finally take my seat next to the most high. Cowardly of me, perhaps, but it affords me some space from the others in the room if not from him. He pats my knee. "I'm sorry about Janeeva, Thurava. That was unkind of her."

"I've never known her to be anything else, in truth, so it shouldn't matter." That it does, I dare not say aloud.

"Still. She shouldn't let her history with your mother bleed into her conduct with you."

"Perhaps she's just getting used to life in Miravat. It's a big change for all of us."

"Yes, but you're too generous to give her an excuse for her behavior."

I lift a shoulder. "Bravlat's words were punishment enough."

The most high hums in agreement. "Especially since they were true. Don't look so shocked. The liaisons made it clear Astrava's elders have nothing material to contribute to the city. Janeeva, like me and the others, must grow accustomed to a life of lesser import."

"Then that is Miravat's loss."

He smiles and tips his head in acknowledgement. "Don't let an old man's complaints eclipse the opportunities the city has for you, my dear. You've always been a star of Astrava. We all want you to shine brightly here."

I will. I must. I have to hope the pain in my heart will fade in time like the Joyful One teaches us.

"Have you thought what your path here might look like?"

"A little." I tell him of my plans to become a lorist.

He looks pleased with the news. "You honor your mother and the rest of Astrava with such a choice, Thurava. But don't let the city distract you from what you truly need."

I think of the spacious upper city apartments. Clothes that flutter on the breeze and shimmer like the feathers of an exotic bird. Mouthwatering foods that leave me hungry for more instead of sated like the communal platters around Astravan cookfires. But like the Great Navigator who traveled the world only to find what they were looking for back home, I'm not enticed by what Miravat has to offer.

"I only want to see the stars."

The liaison standing next to the most high shudders into motion, the smooth face orienting on me. "You should visit the library in the upper city. Your reckoner can take you there."

I know about libraries. I've read of the wondrous buildings full of books that existed before the Great Scatter. Ones my people built and others they collected that captured every conceivable kind of knowledge. That's why I'm confused when my reckoner directs me to the beautiful structure off an upper city plaza full of tables and benches but no books. No shelves along the walls. Dozens of people flit around the room, their hushed words like the soft chatter of the Najimov every spring.

"Why is it so empty?" I speak quietly, but my voice still bounces off all the hard surfaces. Self-conscious, I walk toward an empty alcove that overlooks the street.

"There are currently thirty-one individuals in the library."

"Not people. *Books*." In Astrava, we had dozens of texts, many passed down from before the Great Scatter. Some were typed on thin, cramped pages. Others written lovingly in script documenting our history and that of the stars, bound in lucerva hide. I should ask the most high what happened to them when we left.

The reckoner's silent so long, I wonder if it'll answer. "It is difficult to explain. The Miravat have a technology that places books and other information into the air. When they wish to consult certain books, they can make them appear. See that apparatus near the desk?"

A man pulls a book from a large, crate-like machine with a glassy screen similar to that of my reckoner. "You can make books appear out of the air?"

"We can."

I stare at the plain volume in the man's hands as he goes to a table in the middle of the room. If all books live in the air like the reckoner says, invisible to human eyes, then, "How do you know it's the *right* book?"

"That is a difficult question to answer quickly."

I sigh. The reckoner's said that before in response to other "difficult" questions. "Why did the liaison tell me to come here?"

"Look up."

It takes a moment for the constellations to resolve out of the painting spanning the domed ceiling, and I wonder how I didn't notice the mural when I first entered the room. But then I understand. Instead of a shovel for the Laborer, it's an arrow, a tool of war. The Impulsive One is incorporated into a larger constellation of some sort of birdlike monster similar to the rocs mentioned in old caravan songs. And there are other changes as well.

"These aren't *our* stars."

"No. The people of Miravat have a different cosmology than you from what we have been able to learn of Astrava."

"Cosmology?"

"A way of viewing the world."

The Great Scatter separated our peoples for generations, that much is true, but to have different constellations? "The stars witness our fate as we mark theirs."

"The people of Miravat use the stars to measure the seasons like you, but they do not involve the stars in their daily lives."

"Then how do they know if they're on the right path without the stars' guidance?"

"That is a difficult question to answer quickly."

Perhaps, but it's enough to know the people of Miravat have forgotten the importance of the stars. Something so fundamentally different from us, the implications take my breath away. "Of what use will my stories of the stars be to the people here if I'm to become a lorist?" I ask, half-fearing the answer.

"It will be added to the historical record and help streamline Miravat and Astravan interactions so we can better tailor our explanations for you."

"You view our stories as history?"

The reckoner goes silent.

History's comprised of the past. But Astravans still live, even if not as brightly as we did before. What did Mother say? *We do not turn aside. We bear witness in respect of all that came before.*

My mother pledged to look after our animals. I have no choice but to look after our stories. If I wasn't certain of such a path before, I am now.

On the first day of the month, the reckoner directs me to Kikriva's family's quarters in the lower city. The cramped apartment isn't even half the size of their pavilion in Astrava. Kikriva's mother Zendava weeps happy tears as she pulls me into a hug. Kikriva's father is still at work. Her brother's grown taller and sits in the corner with his reckoner after a curt greeting.

"Kikriva has an errand to run for Devanettu, but don't worry. She'll be back soon." Zendava goes to a pipe in the wall and pours me a cup of water. I watch on avidly. We have similar mechanisms at the lodge, and I've yet to grow tired of watching water instantly appear, no clay vessels or buckets required. She presents the cup to me with a proud flourish. "Come, tell me how you've found the Glass City."

"It's wonderful to be sure, but sometimes it still feels like an ill-fitting shirt." Chafing in all the wrong places.

"Perhaps you only need more time to grow into it."

I hope it's that simple. She gives my clothes—tunic and leggings cut from a shimmery if scratchy yellow cloth—a critical look. The reckoner said they wouldn't immediately announce me as an outsider, but admittedly I hadn't been very concerned about the details.

She tsks and goes to the storage chest along the wall. "I have some of Kikriva's castoffs that will serve you better than what you're wearing."

"I didn't mean to cause offense," I say quickly, still upset I embarrassed my friend in front of her patron. I thought I did better this time.

Zendava waves that off. "The people of Miravat are very particular about clothes. A girl your age must be properly arrayed in public. What you have on now does you no favors. The people here tolerate Astravans, but they fear the lucerva your family tended."

I look up from the pile of dresses. "Is that why they forbade us from bringing them here?"

She nods. "The animals make the people very sick. That's why they took all our clothes away and anything else made from their fur or hide." She grimaces. "And that's also why we must work twice as hard to take extra care with our appearances to ensure we don't remind them of our history with the animals as sometimes their fear can override sense."

Despite the precautions we've taken in learning Miravat's customs, Keevat, one of the boys, had come back to the lodge with cuts and bruises one afternoon. He refused to say what happened or leave the lodge the rest of the week. Had he been a victim of Miravat's fear?

Zurlot looks up from his reckoner. "My teacher says our insides are different from that of the Miravat. Over generations we adapted to living with lucerva, and that's why they don't bother us."

"Or perhaps *they* are the ones who lost the ability to live with lucerva after the Great Scatter," Kikriva's mother says. She leans in to whisper, "His time at school makes him think he's a Truthteller now."

The better part of an hour passes as we swap stories from the seasons we were separated, keeping clear of anything that strays too close to why they left and why we stayed. Zendava gives me a rueful smile. "I'm sorry, Thurava. Kikriva should have been back by now."

"The errand her patron sent her on must be important."

Zendava smiles, relieved. "I'm sure that's it."

I hope so. I hope it's not an excuse to avoid me. But as the day grows late, Kikriva still hasn't appeared. As a child, I spent countless hours in her family's home. But after so many changes between us, I no longer feel comfortable being here, no matter how Zendava tells me my presence is no hardship, that my visit isn't in conflict with any plans she had for the day. When we run out of small talk, I take my leave, despite Zendava's protests.

"Kikriva knows where to find me," I assure her.

As I walk back to the lodge, I wonder if Kikriva actually cares.

In the weeks that follow, my fellow Astravans move out of the lodge and into the city. Some take to their new situation with eagerness, others less so, as they too often accept Laborer positions throughout Miravat. Only Bravlat and a few others receive apprenticeships with the city's craftsmen. They're the first to leave and not look back.

I don't blame them. Although the lodge is surprisingly spacious, it's still located along the outermost ring of the city, and the crumbling masonry, grimy façades, and delicate sewers start to wear after a while. Even the streets are rough with pavers that have buckled up from the ground over time and never been repaired.

And then there's the food. The simple fare the lodge provides cannot compete with the delicacies of the city's market stalls. Fragrant loaves of bread filled with all manner of foods, charred meat on skewers, fruits and nuts I have never seen before, glassy sweets that melt in the mouth, vegetables fried in oil. And spices that always befuddle my tongue and make me crave more. Still, I take most of my meals at the lodge with the remaining elders. Even Janeeva's glower at my presence has transformed into grudging indifference so long as I don't call attention to myself. Thanks to my time on the graze, I'm better prepared for the gruel at breakfast and the simple grain cakes stuffed with vegetables for the midday and evening meals a rotating group of Miravat citizens cook for us each morning before taking their leave.

I'm *not* used to idleness, however, with no lucerva to care for.

One night, with the common room empty of all but me, I take up my staff and go into the city. Even at night, it's too bright to see the stars. Lamps line the streets, their glow chasing away the shadows. Shops are closed for the evening, and lights twinkle from the apartments overhead. Only the occasional tavern is open for business, bawdy laughter and music announcing their presence well before I pass by. The quiet streets are almost soothing after the din of the daytime. My mind's my own again, not so easily distracted by the city's wonders. If I look past the shimmering surfaces, the sights new and strange, I can make out the older parts of the city fashioned from traditional stonework that the newer sections have been built on top of. Generations before, the Miravat were known for their work with rock and metal, and that legacy still shines through.

The hush of the upper city settles over me like a cloak, but it's still much too bright. "Take me somewhere I can see the stars," I tell the reckoner.

It directs me past silent buildings, beyond even the library, leading me to the northern edge where the waters of the Najimov first greet the city. The reckoner said the stars are visible here, and I want only to see them. A small terrace looks across the desert, flanked by two buildings that block the rest of the view. But above, in the distance, where the city's glow gives way to darkness, I can just make out the start of the Impulsive One.

I wasn't very impulsive growing up, not with the responsibilities Mother instilled in me from a young age, but tonight, I fear I'm doomed to forever seek purchase in this strange place, never to find my true purpose in the Glass City. And yet, I lift my face to the stars. What else can I do?

A shout ripples through the night air, followed by a harsh voice speaking in Miravat. A voice directed at me.

I push away from the railing, finding two elegantly dressed young men and a young woman watching me. The reckoner makes sense of their words. "What business do you have here?" the woman demands. The assumption I don't otherwise belong in the upper city needs no translation.

"I came to see the stars." It feels like forever as the reckoner repeats my words to them in tinny Miravat. Plenty of time for me to see the aggressive dislike reflected off their faces. I've encountered enough citizens at this point to not be surprised. But that's always been during the day, with dozens of others around. In this quiet corner of the upper city, not even a liaison sleeps nearby.

"She's one of them, look." The first man points to my staff, the prominent knob of lucerva bone.

"Dirty thing," the woman says with a hiccupping giggle before raising her long sleeve to protect the lower half of her face.

Irritation rises up. Even in one of Kikriva's borrowed dresses I still don't belong in this city.

The first man makes no move to cover his nose or mouth as his gaze rakes over me. When I don't flinch, he comes close enough to grab my staff. That must be key to whatever proves I'm not one of them.

I yank it back. "Leave me alone." The reckoner translates as I stare him down, my staff reassuringly firm in my hands.

"We only want to get a look at you, Astravan." He steps toward me, and I realize his partner's circled around my other side. He makes a grab for my staff again and holds on long enough I catch a whiff of his ale-soaked breath. "The liaisons say you must be welcome here. We want to know why."

The woman titters behind her sleeve, plucks the fabric of my dress, and rolls it between her fingers, making a strange sort of clucking sound. When she reaches for my braid, I drop the reckoner, the chain around my neck snapping taut with its weight, and take up my staff in both hands, no longer interested in conversation that disguises their intentions.

The first man says something that makes the others laugh. But my attention's on their bodies, the release of tension that tells me when they're about to lash out. I smack the one on the left in the shoulder, pivoting to catch the other in the knees, then I'm running, my feet light over the stone tiles, terrified, yet exhilarated by the cool air streaming around me. It's been too long since I've greeted the night like this.

The woman squawks indignantly, then starts to scream. The men's muffled shouts and heavy footfalls follow after me as I leave the upper city behind. If Kikriva's patron was upset by a small breach in protocol when I first called on her, I'm certain she wouldn't be happy to shelter me now. And I dare not consult the reckoner. Soon enough, I'm lost amongst the buildings looming overhead, not recognizing the store-fronts or street intersections. A ghostly glimmer shrouds every surface.

But at least I'm alone, with only the murmur of water on the air. I follow it, thinking I might find the Najimov and be able to get my bearings, my staff tapping with each step I take over the stone cobbles.

I can smell the water before I see it. Humidity pricks against my skin. I expect the serpentine banks of the Najimov or fountains and flowers, not the sight that greets me. Rows upon rows of all manner of plants suspended in open irrigation channels radiating out from a central mechanism that gurgles and groans and pushes the water around.

"What is this place?"

"The city's water garden," my reckoner tells me.

"What kind of plants are these?"

"The vegetables, fruits, and grains that keep the city fed." At its words, a breeze picks up, bringing with it the ripe scent of berries.

"But there's no soil."

"The plants do not need it."

But they need water, and lots of it. During the day, with the sun overhead, even more will be burned up. No wonder the Najimov's suffered so.

"Given the region's poor soil composition and the large population the city supports, the water garden is the best way to grow food."

For Miravat, perhaps. No one else.

In Astrava, we grew our grain and vegetables along the banks of the river. Further south, the Karnez used irrigation channels to water their fields and orchards, but I've never heard of anyone growing crops directly in the water until now.

As the reckoner guides me back to the Astrava lodge, the approaching dawn haunting my steps, I doubt whether I can do what I promised my mother. Give up the ways of Astrava and start over like the Great Navigator did when they left to travel the world. But no matter where they went, they never forgot who they were. Here, in the Glass City, I fear waking up one day a stranger, so entranced by my surroundings, questions as to what lie beneath forgotten.

The most high surprises me when I return, already awake and seated at the common room table. "And where have you been, Thurava?" he asks. "I'm certain your mother wouldn't be pleased with me if she knew you were wandering the Glass City at all hours."

He means to be teasing, but I'm in no mood. "I needed to clear my head, taste the night air. I lost track of time."

"Ah. Grown restless have you? In truth, I'm surprised it's taken this long."

"My time's never been my own for this long." I spread out my hands. "There was always something I could help with in Astrava or on the graze. Here . . . "

"You haven't heard back from the academy yet?"

I shake my head.

"Well, it's no hardship for you to continue on at the lodge until you do."

That may be true, but my shoulders tense up at the thought. "For that to work, I'll need to find *something* to fill up my days."

He gives me a wistful smile. "I'm sorry we elders cannot be better company for you. Too many of us have forgotten what it's like to be young."

"Never apologize for a life well lived." My eyes widen. That's it. "In fact, I don't see any reason why I cannot start my training as a lorist now."

"What do you mean?"

"Why not start now by collecting our stories?" And all the better to do so while Astrava's still fresh in our hearts. "I've been meaning to ask what happened to the books from the elder's pavilion."

The most high's face closes up with a frown. "The ones we were able to bring here I'll have delivered to your room. But . . . "

"The ones bound in lucerva hide?" I ask, half-fearing the answer.

"Those your mother holds in trust for us."

Still a huge loss for all of us. My chest hurts just thinking about it. But at least there's no question my work as a lorist is needed. May it not only preserve our stories of Astrava but also who I am—who we all are—at this moment in our history.

"I'm glad you'll be speaking to the others. Let them tell you their stories of Astrava. You've spent too much time alone these past few weeks, I fear."

"I didn't want to get in the way." Not while the families here made plans to start anew. My presence would only cast a long shadow over them of our old lives in Astrava at a time when they needed to be looking to their futures in Miravat.

The most high pats my hand. "Never be afraid to take your place amongst us. Not even the stars can escape their positions in the sky."

## V. The Truthteller

The next morning, I ask my reckoner for pen and parchment. "You can find such implements at the market. However, that would constitute a significant outlay of credits." Such supplies were precious things in Astrava as well but somehow Mother made sure I had practice with them when I outgrew the slates given to all the children. "Given your current balance, I do not recommend making this purchase."

"How can I collect our stories if there's no way to write them down?" I'd gladly forgo buying anything else if I could do this much for my people.

"I am capable of capturing what is spoken to you and converting it into text, just like I do when I help translate other people's words for you. Would that suffice?"

"Would the stories live in you, reckoner? Like the books in Miravat's library live in the air?"

It flashes for a long moment. "Yes, that is one way to think about it. I can store the stories on this device and call them forth whenever you want. Once the collection is to your liking, we could explore having physical copies made."

That way every Astravan could one day have their own collection of our stories. "I'd like that. Thank you."

And so I tell my reckoner the stories my mother told me. The stories full of fond memories or spoken to me out of irritation. Ones that taught me something about our work or myself or the stars overhead and the lands their light touch.

Then I repeat the stories Rakravat and Linarv shared with me around the fire on the graze or during chores in the lucerva pens. Ones to instruct, to give comfort, to call forth a smile or a peal of childish laughter. Ones where the details have grown blurry with time, others still so sharp in my memory, they've carved an indelible path into my life.

I speak to my reckoner until my voice grows hoarse and the day grows long. Too many stories are incomplete, but they're mine: the ones that have made me who I am and the ones that give me comfort for the times when I cannot have starlight.

At the most high's suggestion, I speak with the elders who remain at the Astrava lodge. About their lives, about which stories they hold in their hearts, about what Astrava means to them. What it should mean going forward.

All good practice for when I start my studies as a lorist. My nerves at speaking with the elders dissipate after the first couple conversations. I never had much interaction with the council members growing up. Even once Mother was named an elder herself, I wasn't privy to the goings-on of the council, but I could always tell when she was fuming over one of their decisions.

The most high suggests I also speak not just with the elders but also the Astravans who've made their way in the city. He gives the liaison stationed in the common room a hard look and beckons me to join him in the hallway. "While you're there, I'd like to know how they're getting on in their new positions."

"Surely they'd tell us if there were problems."

"Perhaps." His brow lowers as he formulates his next words. "But you know better than anyone how being forced into a situation not of your making can change things. If any of our people need us to advocate on their behalf, I would know it."

Would that he'd done more of that *before* our arrival in this city. He must see some of the doubt on my face, for he gives me a pointed look. "The city promised to work with us in good faith."

"Do their promises measure up to ours?" I challenge.

"They know the weight we place on such things. If there's cause, I'll ensure they remember *all* the promises they made to us."

If nothing else, it's a good excuse to leave the lodge, giving my footsteps purpose through the city. I make my way through the crowds, my reckoner leading me toward the outskirts of the factory district. The Astravans I speak with tell me of the monotony of their work, the vague sense of disaffection plaguing them, but most are content at the possibilities of a new life forged on equal footing with Miravat's citizens. I move on, spying Bravlat's graying head through the window of a small workshop on a bustling side street and give it a tap with my staff.

With a start, he looks up from his workbench. His face breaks into a smile warm with recognition. He wipes his hands on a greasy rag and gets to his feet, saying something to the liaison stationed in the room. He opens the door for me. "Thurava, what a pleasant surprise."

"I came to see how you're settling in."

He turns back to the liaison. "I'm taking my break now." To me, "Let's walk a bit. There's a park not too far from here."

I fall into step beside him, telling him of my work to collect our stories while I wait for my acceptance to the academy.

"Your mother would be proud of you, Thurava."

I hope so. I don't know what else to do, in truth. We turn down another street, and there's the promised park. Flowering shrubs in raised beds and low-growing trees fill a city square. Bravlat points out an empty bench near the fountain, splashing merrily. The sound soothes me despite knowing where the water comes from and how hard it's used by this city.

We take our seats. "So tell me, how's the work?"

Bravlat slaps his knee and sits a little straighter. "Well enough, I suppose. We found a nice apartment not far from here."

"That's wonderful." While not the upper city, this is a clean, prosperous neighborhood.

"The work's interesting, too. They want me to inspect the tools and machinery they manufacture and come up with improvements."

"I'm glad to hear they're taking advantage of your skills." Too many others have had to settle with Laborer positions and the drudgery that comes with them.

Bravlat nods. "I just wish I understood their manufacturing processes better. That way I'd know whether my suggestions are even possible in the first place."

"What's preventing you?"

Bravlat grimaces and gives the park a surreptitious glance. "Apparently that's information only the liaisons have. *They* are the ones who authorize what work goes on at which factory, which workers work where, rotating them as necessary so no one can see the whole of what's being done." He shakes his head, frustration tinged with wonder. "When the most high charged me to dismantle the liaison that first came to Astrava all those years ago, I never understood what could account for the regularity I found in the clockwork and circuitry, things that shouldn't have been possible since the Great Scatter."

This happened before I was born, but I well remember how the metal Bravlat harvested from the liaison was the whole of our stores for a long time. He'd pronounced the liaisons creations of forgotten technology from the age before, which threw negotiations into disarray.

"And now that I'm here in this place, following their instructions . . . " Bravlat scrubs his face with his palm.

"They're still machines, no matter how impressive their construction."

Bravlat snorts. "And yet their control over this city is undeniable." He turns toward me. "One of the men who worked here when I first arrived said the reflected light throughout Miravat is not for our benefit but to help the liaisons navigate the city."

When I was younger, the children used to dare each other to creep up behind the liaison where it was so often stationed near the elders' pavilion, seeing how long it'd take before it noticed us. "I knew their peripheral vision was poor . . . "

"Yes. I almost didn't credit what he said, but then I remembered how there were no eyes or anything other than wires and gears underneath their faceplates." A family walks by, and we watch them go past in silence. "But one thing is clear," Bravlat continues in a hard voice, so at odds with his usual good nature. "They don't think like us, Thurava. They don't see or hear like us. In some ways, I believe they're more dependent on us to understand their surroundings than we are on them."

"That would explain the city's design then." The improvements interpreted and doled out by a machine instead of human heads and hands. If they're responsible for Miravat's growth, perhaps that's why it appears so strange to our eyes. "What else did your colleague have to say?"

"That's just it. He was reassigned after our conversation."

My eyes widen. "Were you within a liaison's hearing when you two spoke?"

A grim nod. "I feel guilty for sharing it with you, but you deserve to know. Take care with this knowledge, Thurava."

"I will. And I hope you continue to find your work fulfilling despite such. . . limitations. The liaison stationed at your workshop hasn't given you any trouble?"

He shakes his head.

"If you have any problems, you have only to tell me." I would be a friend to Bravlat and his family even before our journey to Miravat, but now I wouldn't hesitate to see the scales between us balanced after the kindness he's shown me here. "The most high's vowed to intervene if there are any problems with our people in this place."

He smiles in return, but there's no warmth in his expression. "If there ever is, it won't be our doing."

My collection of stories grows with each person I speak with. While the details differ depending on the teller, so much of the framework's the same. Another thread tying us together even though we no longer stand on Astravan soil.

That warms me whenever thoughts of my family intrude on the fragile routine I've found here.

Janeeva approaches me one day after the midday meal at the lodge. "Well? I think it's about time you spoke with me."

"In truth, I wasn't certain you'd want to," I say carefully.

She waves that off with a careless gesture. "I'm Astravan, same as you. You cannot pick and choose what aspects of our history are worth keeping."

"I meant no offense." But I did hope to avoid spending any more time with her than necessary.

She harrumphs and directs me over to an alcove by a window overlooking the street. "Where do you want to begin?"

I swallow my nerves. Since Janeeva's decided to be agreeable, it's best to take advantage of it. "I'd like to know about your life before you were named to the council." I ask my reckoner to collect her words for me.

She frowns to herself, thinking. "I come from a long line of potters. Every dish, bowl, and pot in Astrava came from hands such as these." She raises them up, the fingers gnarled, the joints still swollen from her time at the wheel.

"Did you enjoy it?"

Her green eyes narrow on my face. "Whatever you've heard from my nephew, pottery's an honorable calling."

"Of course," I say quickly. "I didn't mean to suggest otherwise."

In truth, Rakravat missed his family's work but not enough to leave Mother. I remember nights on the graze where he'd roll clay he found in our travels through his fingers or work it into shapes while Mother and Linarv traded stories around the fire. He made me a clay lucerva once when I was little. I brought the figurine everywhere until it broke years later. I wish I had it still. The city might prohibit lucerva from entering their walls but surely not a replica of the creatures.

Janeeva watches me for a moment. "There's something magical about coaxing clay into crockery. I was saddened when I could no longer work as I wished." But she made up for that with her years of service on the elder council. Despite the difficulties in dealing with her, no one can deny that.

"Do you have a favorite story of the stars?"

"You're familiar with the Great Navigator's exploits, yes?"

I nod.

"When the Great Navigator left on their travels, they carried with them four clay vessels filled with spring water so they'd always have a reminder of home with them. The first few weeks, the Great Navigator didn't much think on the water they had stored away as they journeyed farther and farther from home."

She speaks to me as if addressing the council, her voice percussive, as though this is a ceremony and not a conversation.

"The companions came to a bridge guarded by a fierce warlord. After much squabbling, the Great Navigator gifted the first vessel to the man, saying the taste of the waters of home was a priceless treasure. The warlord was pleased and let them pass, and so the Great Navigator continued on their way. The second vessel was used to heal one of the Great Navigator's traveling companions when they were poisoned after unknowingly venturing into a besieged town looking for provisions. While only two vessels remained of the original four, the Great Navigator comforted themselves that half as much was better than none at all as they journeyed on."

Janeeva leans forward, her unblinking gaze on me.

"It wasn't until they reached the coast of a strange land where the local water made them violently ill that they opened the third vessel and drank deeply. That night, the Great Navigator was haunted by dreams of home. In all their travels, the longing to return had never been so strong. The next day, the companions reached a new town with a well that didn't make them sick though it never quite quenched the Great Navigator's thirst. Nor did the water in the next town or any of the cities after that.

"One night, the Great Navigator could put off their terrible thirst no longer and drank from the third clay vessel while their traveling companions slept. No matter how much water the Great Navigator drank, the third vessel remained full. And so they continued on their journey, content they could always drink water from home without fear of it running out."

Janeeva stops to rest her voice. I get a cup of water for her and return to her side. She gives it a rueful look before taking a deep gulp. "You know the rest?"

I give her a tentative nod. She waves for me to get on with it while she takes another sip. "And so the companions came to a vast mountain range," I say haltingly. "In crossing it, the Great Navigator's caravan toppled down a ravine. The fourth clay vessel was flung out, and it smashed where it landed on a rock. The Great Navigator found a metal container they had gotten in their travels and transferred the water remaining in the third vessel into it, no longer trusting the simple clay vessel to keep it safe. Once the caravan was righted, the Great Navigator and their companions continued on their way as they always did.

"That night, when the Great Navigator got the metal container out to slake their unending thirst, the water was no longer bottomless. They'd drunk it nearly dry with only a few mouthfuls remaining. They put it away, vowing to save the rest no matter what happened. From that night on, they could no longer dream of home."

Janeeva takes over. "The Great Navigator failed to realize it was the clay vessels that kept their water so well, not some magical property of the water itself. The clay carries with it memories of the land, of fire, of the person who created it, keeping its contents safe." Her voice grows fierce. "But treated so carelessly, discarded so easily, the vessel's properties died with it. The water was only as good as its container."

"That's why we always put four vessels in each water cache, in honor of the ones the Great Navigator took on their journey." I add softly, "May we never be without."

Janeeva nods, looking pleased. "It's all too easy to overlook the container for the contents, but both must be respected if expected to last." Her gaze goes to the window. "You're now the container for our stories, Thurava. That's why I would talk with you."

Humbled, I bow my head.

"None of that." Her sharp tone makes me cringe. "Only time will tell if you're worthy of it."

That night, the most high beckons me over to his seat by the common room fireplace. "How was your day, Thurava?"

"Well enough. At this point, I've spoken with nearly all the other Astravans."

"Oh? And what have you learned?"

So many things—too many to summarize even though that's clearly what he wants me to do. "Astrava's much more than any single account can hold."

He nods, pleased. "And yet you must try."

For the first time, the weight of what I've tasked myself reaches me. My shoulders slump forward. To think I could carry the whole of our history alone.

"Astravans have always had to face the future set before them by choosing which of our stories and beliefs should guide them."

"But things get lost." Teachings that may not have much bearing on our situation now but might become invaluable at some point in the future.

"Over time, yes. It's inevitable." He nods to the reckoner around my neck. "Perhaps in your studies you'll learn a better way to preserve what's ours. But for us, it was always a choice of what to keep and what we must relinquish."

"During the Great Scatter, it wasn't a choice but a necessity."

"Any choice implies necessity, even if it's of one's own making, Thurava."

I purse my mouth. Mother made it seem like I had no choice but to come to Miravat, but was there another way I couldn't see at the time?

"What's put in our accounts of the stars was a choice. What books were handed down over the ages, another. What we do with that legacy is now yours."

"Not mine alone. You and the other elders must help."

"Must? No. Choose to? Yes. Just as you choose what to ask us, what aspects of our stories are important enough to save, and what details will be lost to time."

"I'm at Serpent's Fork then, just like this city. However I go forward, my task's impossible."

"What you're forgetting about Serpent's Fork is it's not so much the choice between two equally bad options, but the *commitment* to the choice once made." He sighs. "You cannot help the way of the world, Thurava, but you can help how your actions operate within it."

I can feel Mother's temper rising up inside me. "Then why bother putting on a show of consulting the stars before we left Astrava when you already knew what the people would decide?" What he'd already decided for us?

"Would you believe me if I told you I desperately hoped the stars would have shown us another path? That there was a way out of this mess that didn't mean abandoning our home?" He shakes his head. "If I had any doubts of our course, the stars' silence proved we should go on the best we could, even if that meant crawling to our neighbors to the north."

"Mother said you were preserving the ceremony, even if it was a lie."

"Does a truth become a lie if there's no one left to believe in it?"

I don't know how to answer that. I'm not sure I *want* to know the answer.

"Astrava was only as strong as the people who believed in it. How many families left in your short lifetime? Our collapse was foretold before either you or I were born—it was merely our misfortune to live through it. But we don't turn aside. We bear witness to what came before. That's why we consulted with the stars before we left, even if our fates were sealed."

"You said we always have a choice."

"We do, but when you're responsible for the well-being of others, you'll soon learn how quickly those choices get decided for you."

My hand aches from clenching my staff. I cannot say I'd make the same choices he has, but I understand his point. As always, we must go on the best we can.

"You never told me which of our stories means the most to you." It's as much of a peace offering I can give.

He leans forward. "Tell me, Thurava, what story should I choose? The one that means the most to me in this moment right now? The one that's made me who I am? Or the one I think you're in most need of hearing?"

I've heard variations on all of these from the other elders, though I didn't realize it until now. "That's something only you can decide as all the others did with no input from me."

His eyes twinkle in approval. "Very well. I'm sure Sitarva taught you about Ceaseless Storm." I nod. "Good. Then you know it took thirty days and thirty nights before the storm ended."

"And they found themselves on the other side of the world."

"Yes. Their return journey tested them almost as harshly as the storm." He sits back in his chair and sighs. "Some accounts of their travels speak of famines and floods, raiders and sickness, all endured to bring his father much needed aid. What they don't say is that the son and his men would have surely died fighting if the storm hadn't flung them off course. The only reason they were victorious was thanks to the delay and the fact they approached his father's stronghold from the opposite direction." He folds his hands across his chest. "Now, why do you think I told you that story?"

"As a reminder of all the ways the world can work against you once your course is set."

He tips his head, considering that. "Ah, but I didn't tell you this story for your sake alone, Thurava. Ceaseless Storm taught me there are always complications along the way. Take them in stride, succeed despite them, yes. But never forget that sometimes the answer to a problem might lie in the opposite direction. Something that always served me well in the time since I was named the most high."

The first of the month comes around again, and my reckoner alerts me of Kikriva's standing promise to meet me at her parent's home. I have half a mind to ignore the reminder, but I must remember her trials aren't mine. Her patron prevented me from seeing her last time. I must not let that get in the way of our years-long friendship. Besides, so much has changed, I hunger for Kikriva's advice even now.

Zendava eagerly greets me when I get there, and for a moment, my nerves are set at ease. We barely have a chance to exchange pleasantries when Kikriva arrives, looking harried, but her face brightens when she notices me. "Thurava! It's good to see you again."

Something in my chest lightens. "And you."

"I'm sorry I couldn't make it last time. My responsibilities . . . " She trails off with a shake of her head. "Tell me *everything*." She waves me over to the table and sits across from me.

It's almost like those breathless moments after my return from the graze when we tried to share all that happened while I was away. I talk a little bit about our last days in Astrava, Mother's charge to me, and how I've come to spend my days since my arrival in the Glass City. At some point, Zendava takes Zurlot out to run errands, leaving the two of us alone.

"And have you found a position yet?" Kikriva asks me before I can ask about her work for Devanettu.

"I'm to become a lorist," I say proudly.

A wrinkle appears in Kikriva's brow. "A lorist? Do you think that's wise?"

"It's that or become a Laborer. The reckoner told the academy about me."

"But has the academy responded to you?"

I shake my head.

"Did the reckoner tell you the likelihood of being admitted?"

Again, I shake my head.

Kikriva hisses and stabs her finger toward the reckoner where it rests around my neck, always within reach. "Useless things. Did the reckoner tell you entrance to the academy occurs only once a year? Did it tell you how hard it will be to get approval since you don't speak the language?"

"The reckoner will translate for me."

Kikriva scoffs. "That doesn't matter to *them*."

The people who run the academy? "I'll make them see. I've already made so much progress on my own."

Kikriva makes an exasperated sound in the back of her throat. "It doesn't matter how brightly you shine, Thurava. Not here. All the Miravat care about is wealth, status, and how you can be of use."

"True. The reckoner told me they don't even care about the stars."

She spreads her arms wide. "Who needs the stars when you want for nothing?"

I have no answer for that.

"My friend, I don't mean to discourage you. But open your eyes. Stories of the stars—our stories—have no place here." She reaches across the table to cup my cheek. "Holding onto the past will only bring you pain."

I rise from the table. "And willfully forgetting our traditions is better? Is that what you tell yourself every day you spend in your patron's home?"

Kikriva rears back, but the quick temper I remember from our time in Astrava is gone. In its place, Kikriva wears an expressionless mask. Like so many others here. "I do what I must for my family—there's no dishonor in that." She gets to her feet and walks to the door.

No, there's not. Shamed, I bow my head. "Clearly I still have much to learn."

"May you find your way," Kikriva says stiffly in dismissal.

As I leave, I'm not sure what's more upsetting: that I angered Kikriva again, or that she refused to use the stars' blessing. *Lose your place in the stars, you lose more than your way.* The street wavers in front of me.

Blinking furiously, I look down at the reckoner hanging from my neck like a yoke. "What are the odds I'll be granted entry into the academy?"

"Very low, but they may make an exception for you since you would be the first student from Astrava."

"When will they respond to my petition for entry?"

"Unknown. Rest assured, I will let you know if there is any communication from the admissions committee."

That sounds reasonable, but Kikriva's doubts make me wonder if the reckoner's deliberately leaving out key details like the liaison had about the herd being prohibited from entering the Glass City when the Astravans were deliberating on whether or not we should leave our homes. What's gone so wrong with the people of Miravat after the Great Scatter that they've turned their backs on the stars?

I don't realize I've spoken aloud until the reckoner says, "That is a difficult question to answer quickly."

I blink down at the screen. "Then let us start at the beginning."

# VI. Eternity's Stomach

Once, there was a man with an all-encompassing hunger for something that had no name. He amassed wealth and possessions, a fine wife and family, but it didn't slake his thirst. He went to war with his neighbors, building an army that went on to conquer the world, but still it wasn't enough. His wife came to him one day and asked him what it would take to make him happy. He had no answer. And so he ate her.

He ate his sons and daughters when he could stomach their tears no longer. His household prepared a sumptuous feast to assuage his terrible hunger, which he gobbled up along with the table, chairs, and cutlery. Then he ate the servants and the rest of the furniture, the artwork and statues he'd collected, his steeds and soldiers. He walked the lands he'd conquered and swallowed everything and everyone in sight.

All of it resided in his massive stomach, and, for a moment, he was content. Then he saw a beautiful bird that had escaped his appetite. He lumbered after it, and with a mighty jump, he spread his hands wide. But the bird hung out of reach. The man fell back to land in a spray of tail feathers. His stomach split open, and all the people and objects and animals he'd eaten spewed out and scattered throughout the world on the wind.

As the man died, empty once more, the bird vanished into the clouds. The Astrava landed in an arid valley with their lucerva and knowledge of the stars. The Karnez fell to the southern plains with millstones and seeds. And the Miravat landed in the rocky north with pickaxes and forges. No one could say how long they resided in darkness, so they called it Eternity. Much of what they had from the age before was gone, but they learned to live again, with the stars' blessing.

I was taught the tale of a hunger with no name along with the other children around the Astravan cookfires at a young age. A story of the Great Scatter, yes, but also a warning of wanting more than what you need. A lesson that served us well on the lean land we called home.

But such warnings hadn't mattered in the end, with Astrava disbanded, our future entrusted to the Glass City.

The reckoner shows me how to create a book from the air to explain Miravat's history in terms I can understand. I sit at one of the library's tables and start reading. Miravat's history, like so many others, starts with the darkness following the Great Scatter. The people here didn't have lucerva to support them, only metal tools and techniques to mine the rocky land of its riches. They traveled everywhere except to the south for trading partners since the high desert was too formidable for them to cross. That must be why Astrava was isolated from them for so long. For many years, the Miravat survived on their imported foods and refined their metal and stonework. It's only been in my lifetime that they've aspired to more.

Miravat's story of the Great Scatter is similar to ours, but instead of a cautionary tale, it's become a guiding principle. Miravat citizens believe gathering up anything and everything is a good strategy for survival in case the items prove useful in the future. Such a philosophy makes sense after such a long period of scarcity in the time since the Great Scatter. It also explains why Astravans have been granted entry to the Glass City—we'll be tolerated because the Miravat believe everyone has a use, even if they don't particularly like us.

But that doesn't explain why Miravat's turned their back on the stars.

The reckoner directs me to another book with a similar tale of how the Miravat made a living out of finding metal in the ground and creating wonders out of the rock around them. They traded with peoples to the north and west that I've never heard of for medicines and foodstuffs, their craftsmanship in high demand. But one day, they found something in the ground that was not metal or stone but a strange artifact from the age before. The artifact told them how to build liaisons and how to construct the Glass City and how to gather together people with the expertise to make them the envy of the region.

The Miravat have no need of the stars when the artifact tells them what to do. *Who needs the stars when you want for nothing?* But an artifact from the age before that can raise cities? Is such a thing possible?

"What is this artifact?" I ask the reckoner.

"The Miravat call it the Provider."

"Is it a machine like the liaisons? Like you, reckoner?"

"No. It is beyond mere machinery."

"Where is it?" No one here has ever mentioned such a thing.

"You already met it. Each liaison is connected to it with invisible strings. The people of Miravat make the reckoners as well at its instruction to help streamline interactions across the city."

"So in Astrava, we were communicating with the Provider directly and not the leaders of the Glass City?"

"The leaders of Miravat work together with the Provider. In practice, they are one and the same."

"I don't understand."

"The city council consults with the Provider in all things, including the negotiations with your people."

"We came to you in good faith. If we'd known this Provider was involved—"

The reckoner's screen flashes. "The Provider is very old, from the time when the people were one and capable of wondrous things. It was lost to the world until the Miravat uncovered it. Grateful for being rediscovered, the Provider helped the Miravat become what they are today."

That must have been the moment the Glass City was born. A star in ascendance. And—also—when Astrava began to wane.

I shake my head. "Miravat's advancements have cost Astravans their home." All our negotiations hadn't mattered in the end. A show to placate us. Like the most high when he told us to consult the stars, even though he knew they wouldn't speak to us no matter how brightly our pyre blazed.

"Greatness has a cost. The Provider has done what it can to gather you to the Glass City and give you a new home."

"But not the lucerva, not the very things that have defined us for generations."

"The Provider cannot weigh the needs of the few over that of the many."

"And you, reckoner? Do you spy on me like the liaisons for the Provider?"

"I am a gift from the Provider, but I am also your legal advocate."

I remember that term from when I was first given the reckoner. "What does that mean?"

"I am to help you in all matters that are lawful without interference from the Provider or anyone else."

"Why?"

"That is a difficult question to answer quickly."

"Try."

The screen flashes for a long moment. Thinking. "The Provider wants all its children to succeed. Sometimes this requires instruction, sometimes suggestion, and sometimes the space to grow into what cannot be predicted."

"I'm not the Provider's child. I'm Thurava, daughter of Sitarva, daughter of Vachava and the noble Astravans before her."

"You dwell in Miravat at the Provider's behest. The Provider is nothing without people like you to care for."

"I would see it."

"The liaisons—"

"*No*. I would see the true Provider, this artifact that can create cities where there were none before."

"Shh!" A Miravat citizen glares at me from his table across the room.

I clench my fists and take a deep breath. He probably cannot follow our conversation no matter how loud, but I endeavor to speak more quietly. I prod my reckoner. "Well?"

"That is not customary, Thurava."

"Why not?" I would think everyone in Miravat would want to know who or what their benefactor is.

"The Provider chooses who it reveals itself to like members of the city council and others it deems important."

"And I'm not important here." A lesson I've learned over and over again since my arrival in the Glass City.

"That is not true. You have your use as does any other citizen. The difference is most people are content to not concern themselves with such things."

Because they want for nothing. Because the Provider's found a way to bring the world to this rocky plain and keep everyone here content.

"Then why show me these books when the people of Miravat don't even know their own history?"

"Because you asked."

And the reckoner's charged with helping me in all lawful matters without outside interference.

Biting my lip, I consider the blank screen before me. "Please pass on my request to the Provider. I don't care if it's not customary or goes against Miravat protocols. I am Astravan, and I would see what governs me."

"Your formal request for an audience has been sent. The Provider handles many simultaneous processes in caring for the city. Do not take offense if it does not respond quickly."

Much like my petition to the academy, I fear.

I collect my things and leave the library. On the street, sunlight sparkles in every direction. A glamour much like the one the Provider's cast over this city and its people, preventing us from taking a deeper look. Unspent energy coils through me. I have no chores, no miles to hike, no one to share in the truths I've just uncovered. I need to do something or I'll ignite from the inside like a dying star.

I grip the reckoner firmly. "Where does the city council meet?"

"They convene in the council chambers across the plaza." There, a large building rivaling even that of the library gleams in the sun, thanks to the unique gray-white stone that makes up its façade. "But the afternoon session is closed to the public."

"Understood." But I don't alter my trajectory as I march across the plaza and force open the massive wooden doors to the chambers.

A small atrium is empty save for one liaison stationed along the wall. It wakes as I stride past it. "This meeting is closed to the public," it calls after me.

Inside, a large table is set on a dais that comprises the back third of the room. Council members are seated around it—men and women both. The rest of the space is filled with benches for times when they allow an audience in here.

"My name's Thurava of Astrava, and I seek an audience with the council." I brandish the reckoner before me like a shield as it translates my words.

The council members break out in alarmed voices. I don't know what they're saying. I don't much care. I only know of the words inside me, desperate to claw their way out.

"We thought we dealt with you on equal footing. Why didn't you tell us of the machine that governs you?"

The liaison takes me by the arm, and my reckoner drops from my hands, the chain around my neck jerking it against my chest once more. I keep my spine straight, my grip firm on my staff as I'm escorted out of the building.

An elderly woman, one of the council members, comes with us. She has smooth brown skin, wide-set brown eyes, and light gray hair cut short. She and the liaison speak briefly about what to do with me. Whatever the liaison recommends, she waves off. She places the reckoner back into my hands so I can see her translated words. "Thurava, is it? It must be difficult for you to have left your home to come here."

"We Astravans are used to difficulties, lady. Not lies."

Her eyes widen once the translation reaches her. "We don't deal in lies, but clearly we haven't adequately communicated our society's rules to you." Her brows crease together. "The liaisons—"

"You mean the Provider's spies?"

"The Provider helped us build this city and tends to our needs. It doesn't spy on us but watches us grow." She shakes her head in exasperation. "How did you even come to ask such questions?"

"We might have been brought here under false pretenses, but I would know the truth of this city now."

"Your grief for Astrava has fueled your unfair judgments against us, against the city." She eyes my staff, and my shoulders draw back. "You're desperate for any reason to go back to the world you know. Your people were once great visionaries, but I don't see any of that legacy now."

Her words flicker over me like lightning. "We aren't what we once were—no one is—but at least any greatness we once had cannot be attributed to a machine."

"Oh no. The Provider is so much more than a machine. *It* is everywhere." She sighs. "How can I make you see?" She takes my reckoner and inputs an unfamiliar sequence of commands. "There. Next week, I've authorized a time for you to meet the Provider. Your reckoner will ensure you make your appointment."

She looks me over as if not quite knowing what to do with me. I've weathered that look too often from Mother. "I'm sorry this is such a difficult time for you. Given the circumstances, I've asked for clemency in dealing with your disruptive behavior. Another infraction, and my hands will be tied."

I give her a tight nod. Ungrateful of me perhaps, but I cannot speak over the tears crowding my throat.

"Go well." She returns to the council chambers with a swish of her robes.

The liaison stirs at my side. "You must go back to the Astravan lodge. There you will stay until your audience with the Provider."

Confined to quarters? Clemency for anyone except me.

When I reach the lodge, the liaison at my side, the most high gets to his feet. "What happened?"

The liaison steps forward before I can answer. "Thurava of Astrava must stay here for the next five days as punishment for disrupting a city council meeting." If I didn't know better, I'd say it sounds disappointed. "If she leaves the lodge in that time, you will all be held accountable."

"I'd never put my people in such a position," I say indignantly, but the liaison's expression doesn't change.

Over the surprised murmurs of the others, it backs out of the building and lumbers down the street. One of the elders shuts the door behind it.

The most high turns to me in alarm. "Thurava?"

Part of me quails at the attention. The rest stands firm, at peace with the actions I've taken this day. "It's as the liaison said. I'm not allowed to go into the city for the next five days. All because I put questions to the city council they didn't wish to hear."

The most high frowns, his bushy brows lowered in thought. "But such a punishment . . . "

"I earned it because I wouldn't wait for the public session tomorrow."

Janeeva harrumphs. "You forget how your actions reflect on all of us. So like your mother, thinking you're better than the rest of us."

She's somehow managed to combine every one of my secret pains into something monstrous, conjuring forth a twisted version of myself with just her words. I may have lost my family, my flock, my future as a lorist, but I can no longer tolerate her slander against Mother.

"My *mother* is more honorable than every person in this room. She's the only one of us who truly understands what it means to be Astravan. Her sacrifices are what allow us to be here with a clear conscience. Never forget that, Janeeva of the bitter tongue. Your lies will never find purchase if you go against the stars."

I hold her gaze as she glares at me, her cheeks tinted purple with her temper.

"Besides," I continue, "I'd think we should all be worried that a strange machine from the age before is the real power in this city." I tell them about the Provider, the unnatural extensions of itself created through liaisons and reckoners. Not simple clockwork as we assumed but sophisticated machinery with a guiding hand behind it.

For the first time, the most high looks worried. "You saw this Provider then?"

"No. But I will the day my confinement ends."

More mutterings break out. The most high raises his voice. "There's nothing to worry about. We can only wait until Thurava's audience with this Provider. In the meantime, we have food, a safe place to stay, and each other, yes?" He pats my hand. "And if nothing else, you'll have plenty of time to continue your studies to become a lorist over the next few days."

I inhale sharply at that, recalling my argument with Kikriva, the truth of her words now painfully clear.

The most high's eyes widen. "What's wrong?"

"That's not to be, I'm afraid." I keep a firm grip on my staff. I need all its strength now. "I learned my reckoner . . . misrepresented the process of entry into Miravat's academy. The odds are such I'll need to look elsewhere for a position."

The resulting shocked whispers don't hurt nearly as much as Janeeva's smug grin. I don't even need her to speak—I already well know what she's thinking. How it serves me right for putting myself above the honest work so many of our people had to accept, how such a setback can only hurt Mother's charge to me, the true target of so much hate.

*You're now the container for our stories, Thurava. Only time will tell if you're worthy of it.*

After what's happened, I fear shame is all I'm fit to contain. Even the most high, always unflappable, has no response to the news. Some disappointments in life not even the stars can help us navigate. Those are the times we must look within.

I take a deep breath, my gaze touching all the assembled faces. "It's all right. I still have our collection of stories. I'll find a way to see them preserved, even if I have to do it without this city's help."

The weight of such a promise settles over the room, but it's mine to make and now mine to keep, whatever happens.

The most high gives me a sober nod. "So you will, little star. So you will."

The day of my audience with the Provider, I forgo my morning meal with the others and set out into the city. Its familiar glare is almost a comfort. Well-fortified with my staff and the marking stone in my pocket, I make my way to the upper city. Instead of directing me to the city council as expected, my reckoner takes me back to the library. For the first time, the staid atmosphere, instead of suffusing the air with possibilities, sends prickles along my spine sharp with foreboding.

"I thought I was to meet the Provider today."

"You are. See the liaison beside the wall? It will escort you down to the lower level of the library."

At the reckoner's words, the liaison beckons me toward a door that looks like it's been cut from stone. I never noticed it before. As I go down the curved stairs, lights embedded in the smooth walls illuminate my passage. Humidity slickens the treads under my feet. The deeper I go, the more aware I become of the rock around me, over me, pressing so close I'm surprised the liaison is able to follow me down as nimbly as it does.

At last, I reach the bottom. A low roar fills the chamber but it's the soft glow coming from the large, boulder-sized object stationed in the center of the room that commands my attention.

Water rushes through small stone channels in the floor, the metal grating over top gleaming dully. The channels converge on the strange object, casting steam into the air. Being in this place sets me on edge, as if the tiny gnats that always pester the lucerva during the days of long sun are suddenly crawling underneath my skin.

I pick a careful path over the water channels. "*This* is the Provider?"

"Yes," the liaison answers from its place by the doorway. It walks toward me slowly. I know that pace—I've used it myself when approaching a wounded lucerva, not wanting to startle it and cause more harm than good. "It contains knowledge of what was lost in the Great Scatter. But it may as well be rock without your kind to make use of its stores."

And the people of Miravat would never willingly throw away something that could be of use.

The liaison clicks and whirrs, but I can barely make it out over the rushing water. "Even in the age before, the Provider was something rare and wonderful."

"And what of the liaisons' purpose then? To keep us at a remove from the Provider's knowledge yet ensure the city still benefits from it?"

"That is one of our directives, yes."

"And why liaisons control so much of the city."

"They are extensions of the Provider."

It's always strange speaking with liaisons, and doubly so now that this one speaks for the inanimate rock beside me. I try to peer past the glow that sets the artifact's tan surface to gleaming. It beckons me to touch it. It's blazing. I yelp and pull my hand back.

"Water from the Najimov is required to keep the Provider cool, and the resulting steam helps power this building and others across the city." The liaison gestures to a section along the far wall full of twisting pipes, countless gauges, and tiny lights that flash red and yellow through the fog.

"Yet another reason why the Najimov's gotten so low," I grumble.

"The Provider only borrows the water for a time, then shares it with the rest of the city. But an increase in residents means the city requires more water to meet their needs. You have seen the water garden, yes?"

I nod.

"Miravat has gathered people from all over." The liaison spreads its spindly arms in apology. "We did not anticipate our water needs would so negatively affect the region. We made adjustments to keep the Najimov flowing by securing an underground source of water."

The same water source that feeds the desert creepers, which in turn feed the lucerva and Astrava after that. *Mother.* A lump forms in my throat. Navigating the desert with the herd will be all but impossible without vitav to sustain the animals. Water caches won't be enough.

"The Provider's knowledge of what once was is undeniable," I say slowly, "but you know nothing of the damage you've wrought beyond Miravat."

"The Provider has only endeavored to bring the world to the people of Miravat. What lies beyond the city's walls has not been a priority before now."

*They don't think like us, Thurava. They don't see or hear like us. Take care with this knowledge.*

Why should I expect something made of metal gears to care of human concerns? My grip on my staff grows slick, and my clothes stick to my back and sides. Beads of condensation appear on the liaison's carapace. I swallow the compulsion to flee this room and wipe away any trace of the Provider from my body.

The liaison's voice changes slightly, as though coming from a deeper part of its machinery. "Do my answers disappoint you, Thurava?"

I glare at the Provider, feeling the liaison's unblinking attention on me.

"I have let you roam my city." The liaison continues to speak on behalf of the Provider. "I have let you see all the good work we have done, the wonders created here and shared with the rest of the world, and yet you are still unsatisfied."

The liaisons stationed around the city, spying on my movements, the people I spoke with, always watching—and listening too, no doubt. Bravlat's prudence during our conversation that day in the park showed me the risks, but such deception's never come easy to me.

"You may have given my people refuge, but *you're* the one responsible for our troubles in the first place. How could I ever be comforted knowing that?"

For a moment, only the chugging surge of water fills the room. "What do you know of your people's history from the age before?"

It's as though the Provider was sitting beside me as I spoke with the others, collected what was left of Astrava, and found it wanting. My reckoner was with me. Perhaps it was.

No. The reckoner said it's my legal advocate. It cannot have two masters, can it?

"We were capable of great things," I finally say. Words that only scratch the surface of our accomplishments, but I won't justify my people—or myself—to the Provider.

"So very many things, Thurava. The people of Miravat always marvel at the fact their provincial neighbors to the south were once a part of a great civilization that presided over the world. And your people traded it all for the stench of smoke and lucerva dung."

"The Great Scatter's to blame for that," I say sharply.

"Are you so sure?"

I'm not. And somehow this . . . this *thing* knows that. "I've been working to preserve Astrava's stories and its history as we know it. Though much of what we'd already documented we couldn't bring into the city thanks to your ban on lucerva."

"My library stores are available to you as you already know." My mind cannot help but cast the liaison's words in a dismissive tone.

"That hardly makes up for the destruction of our way of life."

"Change is inevitable if your people are to become what you once were."

For a moment, I stand torn. How many times did Kikriva and I imagine we lived in the age before to escape the realities of the harsh sun shining down or bellies never quite full? When the most high and the other elders shared our stories, telling us all the unbelievable things our people had done before the Great Scatter dashed them to pieces, I remember wondering why it must be us who suffer simply by virtue of being born when we were. Those same stories, while capturing our amazing history, also showed how impossible it is to try and recreate what the Astrava once had.

Too much has been lost. We cannot simply pick up where we left off, can we? There's a yawning gulf between what happened and what we have now. Even if we tried, could we ever trust an artifact from Miravat in such an endeavor?

"We've always done our best to shine to our fullest," I say slowly, "but—"

"The Astrava never had the opportunity to consider the possibility of another path, until now," the liaison—no, the Provider—interrupts.

"A path *you* forced us into."

"Unforeseen circumstances," it says as if Astrava's destruction was merely an inconvenience. "We have done our best to make amends and are prepared to help you in this too."

By luring Astravans to the Glass City. If I wasn't certain before, I'm certain now that Kikriva's messages were deliberately kept from me. Probably those from the others as well. All to maintain the Provider's control over us and tempt us ever closer. Some chose this place with clear eyes, but the others . . . The most high sitting in the Astrava lodge's common room, his wisdom and leadership a resource gone to rot like meat left out in the sun. And me? I didn't choose this city. Nor am I satisfied with the opportunities available to me. Serpent's Fork, in more ways than one.

"Your actions have hurt those I hold dear. I must warn them." I whirl toward the stairs.

The liaison stands in my path. "You would leave Miravat, knowing what we offer you?" It watches my face, and the artifact at my back sends a wash of cold down my spine. "We know of your desire to become a lorist. We could guarantee your acceptance into the academy by ensuring the human committee does not reject your application."

Making myself even more beholden to it? I shake my head. "I could shine very brightly indeed with your help if I stay. But the sacrifice is too high."

"Once people come to Miravat, we are not accustomed to letting them leave again."

"You won't let me go?" I cannot keep the panic from my voice. The humidity grows oppressive.

"We have taken considerable steps to feed, clothe, and shelter your people in return for your contribution to our society. Contributions you have yet to make, Thurava, uncommitted as you are in your trade." The liaison's inflection doesn't change, but its voice grows more sinister to my ears.

"You've taken what's customary and turned it into a contract. One I didn't realize I'd entered into," I reply slowly. How can I make the Provider understand? The reckoner's weight in my hands turns reassuring when I remember what it told me. "I'm asking you for the space to grow into what cannot be predicted."

Water murmurs and swirls as the liaison contemplates me, its internal components ticking away. After a long moment, the liaison steps back and bows awkwardly in the Astrava fashion of farewell. "Very well, Thurava, daughter of Sitarva. Keep the reckoner as our gift to you. May it be of use, and may you find your way back to Miravat one day."

I don't draw clear breath into my lungs until I find my way outside of the library. The sunlight banishes the slick chill along my skin. I've negotiated with the Provider for my freedom from the Glass City's walls. Now, what to do with it?

The wind picks up, and for a moment, the high desert breathes over me before the familiar scents dissipate. Tears well up in my eyes at how broken everything's become.

Kikriva. I need to talk to Kikriva. She's always helped me see problems with clear eyes and spoken truth even when I didn't wish to hear it.

I tell the reckoner to take me to her patron's house, but as the directions resolve on the screen, I make no move to follow them. Once, I wouldn't hesitate to go to Kikriva with anything. Out of all the others, she's the only one besides Mother and perhaps the most high, who'd understand the magnitude of the deception this city's cloaked itself in. But the last time we spoke . . .

A tear falls onto the screen, and I wipe it off with my sleeve. No, I cannot let any of that stop me. Armed with newfound resolution, I make my way to Devanettu's home. Relief fills me when Kikriva's the one to answer the door. "I must talk with you."

The look of alarm on her face gives me pause. "What are you doing here, Thurava? You know I cannot be—"

"*This* cannot wait."

Kikriva rears back as her patron comes to the door. Devanettu eyes me, and her gaze lands on my staff. "You again?" To Kikriva, "Handle it. *Quickly*. My guests will be arriving any moment."

Kikriva starts to apologize, but Devanettu cuts her off with a slashing gesture of her hand. Kikriva flinches and falls silent. Head lowered in shame, Kikriva's shoulders slump forward as her patron stalks back inside. Kikriva shuts the door behind her and turns her infuriated gaze on me. "You know how crucial this position is to me and to my family. What could possibly be so important to risk all that?"

"You must know what I've learned." I grip her hand. "There's a machine underneath the library controlling the entire city." My voice pitches higher. "When the Najimov was no longer enough, they stole the underground river that feeds the desert."

She shakes me off her, her face tinged with anger. "What are you talking about?"

"Don't you see? They lied to us, about everything. About the liaisons, about our coming here. They even kept your messages from me so they could gather us here."

Kikriva's eyes widen at that, and she begins to pace. "I cannot deal with this right now. Be off with you. You *cannot* be here when Devanettu's guests arrive. Don't force me to choose between you."

Didn't she hear what I said? "But Kikriva—"

"Enough, Thurava. If our friendship means anything to you, you will leave now."

Her words knock the wind from my lungs. But I do what she asks. I take up my staff and leave her to her patron, her position, her perfect life here in Miravat's upper city. No matter what it's cost me or my family, no matter what it's cost every Astravan who cares to be known as such—something that's no longer a certainty.

The wind continues to swirl, carrying me back down to the lower city, still reeling from the knowledge Kikriva's truly lost to me. Mother all but begged me to move on from our friendship, but I was too sentimental to at the time.

I won't make the same mistake again.

I've been in the city so long, I've lost track of the seasons. Time moves differently within Miravat's shimmering walls than without. Comparing the number of days the reckoner has been in my possession to the orientation of the stars, I should find Mother, Linarv, and Rakravat in Astrava on the much-diminished banks of the Najimov. The yeanlings will be born soon, but hopefully there's still time to warn them before the graze casts them into the desert.

I carry as much food as I can manage in my pack and still walk comfortably, knowing my load will only lighten as I travel. With my knowledge of the stars and the locations of the water caches, I should be able to make good time overland. But such optimism is all before my tarp frays in the long, hot sun. Before the first water cache and the second I find are both dry. Then my shoes—a far cry from my sturdy hide boots—start falling apart. Only my staff remains unaffected by the harsh conditions as I tap my way south.

Despite depleting my funds to purchase supplies for my journey, I finally understand the danger the high desert poses. I was too well protected and trained from an early age to realize our days away from Astrava during the graze were the result of generations of handed-down knowledge. Of course, when compared to all that, supplies from the Glass City would be inferior. A harsh lesson.

I trudge toward the Najimov where it slices through the horizon. Following its winding course south to Astrava will take longer, but at least there I can be certain of the water if nothing else.

*Traveling the desert wastes*
*Make haste, make haste*
*Lest the monsters get a taste*
*Of you*

The caravan songs of old are my only companions as I march. I sing them until my throat scrapes raw, the words repeated so many times, they become meaningless syllables.

*Desert skies the roc flies*
*Make your song carry*
*Lest they carry you away*

After all that, I'm still many long nights away from the settlement. The rhythm of the graze thrums in my blood, but my pace outstrips even those long days and nights we spent with the herd on the move. I sleep only a few hours at a time, the rest I spend walking, always moving forward.

One night, my city-dulled instincts flare back to life when a twig snaps somewhere off to my right. I'm no longer alone with only the stars to light my way.

Turning, I keep my staff in front of me and face a thicket of dead scrub left stranded when the river receded. There, with its flat, pointed face peeking out from underneath a low-hanging limb, a nazoph watches me through its yellow-tinged eyes. This one gives up stealth and crawls out its hiding place. It's even smaller than I expected. It must have abandoned its desert territory to be closer to the river. I grip my staff tightly as we glare at one another.

The stars won't let this creature threaten my task here, will they?

The nazoph trills deep in its throat, then launches itself at me. My staff meets it with a hard thump and knocks it back. I barely have time to plant my feet when it attacks again. Its front foot, with claws outstretched, snags my leg, shredding the fabric and shallowly slicing skin. I gasp. Kicking it off me, I brandish my staff and smack the nazoph on the head. My chest heaves with each breath as it scrambles back. The wet hot burn along the outside of my thigh competes for my attention with an inner voice shouting *no* over and over again.

There's no one here to help me. Not Linarv's sharp eyes or Rakravat's bolts. Not Mother with a lifetime of grief coiled within each strike of her staff. I have to be enough. For all of us.

I force my limbs into motion as I advance and swing, bringing the heavy knob of bone topping the staff down onto the creature with a meaty thunk.

It roars. I slam the staff down again, this time catching it along its soft underside. The nazoph squirms away and flees into the brush, an alarmed trill shattering the night air.

I take a step after it, then wince. My leg. Thankfully the cut's stopped bleeding, but I risk reopening it with each stride if I don't take care now. I slip into a defensive crouch as I wrap it tightly with scraps of my torn leggings, my hands certain even as I keep my gaze trained on the scrub just beyond sheltering the wounded nazoph.

I'm very lucky I won this standoff. But the nazoph's behavior, just like its presence along the Najimov, is unusual. The creatures usually fight to the death, as I well know, which is why they're such a concern during the graze. Is it affected by the loss of the underground river that crosses the desert as well? Is nothing certain anymore with the Glass City on the horizon?

I nearly give into the urge to shout my questions to the night sky. Why didn't the stars warn my people? What's preventing them from telling me what to do now? *Looking for patterns where there are none will turn you cross-eyed.* I clench the marking stone of the Great Navigator in my fist, the blood in my veins pushing against its smooth, unyielding surface.

Anger without an outlet is of no use to me. I have to remember my purpose here, the truth I carry, and the knowledge that only I am in a position to warn my mother. Beyond that, I'm at the mercy of the stars.

They sparkle overhead as they always do. That must be comfort enough.

## VII. Dying Star

Linarv sees me first from his post in the outermost pasture. His desperate shout brings Mother and Rakravat running from the lucerva pens as I limp into Astrava. My scalp and shoulders blistered from the sun, my lips wind-burned, and my shoes made from Miravat's finest false leather falling apart at the seams, I wait for my mother to acknowledge me. Joyful recognition flashes across her face like lightning then shifts into a stern sort of concern. Rakravat sweeps me off my feet and bundles me into his arms.

The musky-sweet smell of the lucerva clinging to his shirt brings tears to my eyes as he carries me the rest of the way to the pavilion I once shared with Mother. Still standing. Excepting Linarv and Rakravat's, all the others have been dismantled, leaving only spindly beams and scuffed platforms behind.

"You shouldn't be here," Mother says even as she checks me over for injuries with brisk hands. "Salve and water," she tells Linarv hovering near the pavilion's entrance. "Foolish girl," she says so softly I nearly miss it.

"Not a fool, nor a girl any longer," I croak out. "I must tell you—"

"It will wait." She strips off my clothes and nestles me in the furs of her bed as though I'm a child sick with fever.

I struggle against the blankets, against fatigue so deep in my bones, it's a wonder I still draw breath. Mother's familiar scent surrounds me, so reassuring everything else threatens to slip away. "But—"

"Hush. Drink." Water laced with sleeping weed is forced down my throat. I sputter and drink deeply. Then know no more.

When I wake, there's a moment much like Eternity where I forget Astrava's no more. Where I can live in my memories and pretend the Glass City's only a glimmer on the horizon. Where I don't have to face how far I've fallen, and how much farther I have to go.

Mother stirs beside me, and I can hide no longer. "You're finally awake."

"Yes." Dryness ravages my mouth. "How long—"

"Here. Wait." She helps me sit up and holds a drinking bowl to my lips. I lap the water up like a greedy fish. "Little more than two days." When I finish, she sets the bowl down and pushes the hair back from my face. "You worried us terribly."

Tears burn the corners of my eyes. "I'm sorry. But I have to—"

"It'll wait until Rakravat and Linarv can hear it as well. Tonight."

I've heard that tone from her too many times to protest now. A few hours more. I can wait that long before burdening them with the truth.

"How's the herd?" I ask instead.

"The birthing went well enough. Though one of the females got spooked and trampled one of the yeanlings," she says with a sigh. An accident, surely, but no less painful. "But all told, the stars have smiled upon us this season."

The stars . . . I clear my throat. "The most high told me he left some of our books with you."

"He did." She goes to the trunk at the foot of her sleeping platform. Nestled in a pure white lucerva fur, she pulls out one of them, the pages collected there stacked thicker than my fist. "I've not looked at them since they were left in my care." Her gaze goes distant. "I was angry when everyone left, yes, but it was also too painful to read through them and contemplate all we've lost."

"That's understandable."

She smiles, but it slips away just as easily. "Perhaps, but not when you're supposed to bear witness."

"Something you were never supposed to do alone."

She lifts a shoulder. "I had Rakravat and Linarv with me."

"You could have had me here too." I could never hide anything from her, and I cannot hide my hurt now.

She kneels beside me and takes my hands, her callused palms warm against mine. "Oh, little one. I've missed you." Tears glimmer in her eyes. "It wasn't easy sending you away, but I only wanted what was best for you."

"I know." I'm just sorry when it came to it, I wasn't worthy of her sacrifice or mine.

"I must see to the animals." She gets to her feet, intent on the day's work.

"What can I do to help?"

"You can stay here and rest."

"But—"

"No," she cuts me off. "You very nearly didn't come back to us, Thurava. I won't have you put yourself at risk while you're under my care." She gives me a stern look, until I nod reluctantly. "I'll see you later."

For a moment, I lay there on the sleeping pallet, letting the familiar surroundings settle back over me. Something deep down inside relaxes for the first time in months. No wonder the Great Navigator dreamt of home, when this is what it feels like to return after a long absence. A sense of rightness. Or perhaps it's only the absence of so much of the wrongness that lives behind Miravat's walls.

*We all have a choice, Thurava. To give up, to destroy, or to go on the best we can.* But I refuse to cede any more ground to the Glass City.

"Tell me again," Mother demands.

As she paces, I do as she asks, with Linarv and Rakravat listening on as the fire pops and grumbles beside us. Nights like this never felt lonely on the graze, but here, in what was once Astrava, there are too many ghosts in the air for the familiar surroundings to bring comfort.

"And you fear the underground river that feeds the desert has been redirected at the will of this Provider?" Mother asks when I finish.

"Yes. That's why the grazes have gone so poorly of late. They starved the desert from underneath when the Najimov was no longer enough."

Mother hisses. I know what she's thinking. All those years the elders' council negotiated with the Glass City to protect what little of the Najimov's course they let us have, only for this to happen now. Unimaginable at the time.

"They didn't realize how it would affect you," I offer.

"But that wouldn't have changed their strategy from what you've told us."

I shake my head. Not with all the Provider's children living within the Glass City's walls.

"We are but fodder to the Provider's stomach in its hunger for greatness." Mother looks to Linarv and Rakravat for their reaction to my tidings.

"We could go south," Linarv rumbles softly.

Mother throws up her hands. "And what if it's no better? The Karnez have all but abandoned their territory."

"We could walk the banks of the Najimov," Rakravat offers.

"And what happens when the Provider decides to drain the river completely?" Mother challenges.

The unique silence of the high desert settles around us.

*Never forget that sometimes the answer to a problem might lie in the opposite direction.*

And just like that, I know what needs to be done. "I have a better idea: We take the herd to the Glass City." That's the only real option we have left now. The Provider made it so.

"But they won't admit the lucerva," Mother says.

"Leave that to me. You told me once that we must shine as brightly as we can, no matter what. But with the Astrava no more, we must become the dying star, blazing into glory." I meet each of their gazes. "And the Glass City will bear witness."

Mother insists we wait a few more days before leaving, time enough for my brow to no longer go clammy at the slightest bit of exertion, for my appetite to rival even that of Rakravat's. But once that's behind us, even she can no longer find any excuse to delay our course now it's been set.

I help Rakravat and Linarv gather up the herd, including the new batch of yeanlings that scamper through weeds and scrub but never venture too far away from their mothers. The march north will be particularly difficult on them. Linarv prepares a grain mash to help bulk them up, and we'll carry the excess in clay vessels in case they need it as we travel. Even some of the adolescent males must carry their weight in provisions as we prepare to leave Astrava once more—perhaps for the last time.

Returning's far easier than my departure, now that I'm properly outfitted. Mother leads us each night. I know she doubts much of what I told her of the wonders of Miravat, but her anger runs hot at the manipulation of Astrava. Linarv and Rakravat have always kept their own counsel, but they'll follow Mother until their dying breaths.

Even into the Glass City.

A week later, Mother eyes Miravat's soft glow on the horizon. Dawn's coming, along with the time to rest. Already, the stars are fading from the sky. Only the brightest ones in the constellation of the Joyful One can be spotted, and it's only a matter of time before they too are gone.

Mother sighs and looks at me. "The Joyful One wasn't always joyful, you know."

I've heard the story before, but I won't spoil an opportunity to hear her tell it. I have to tamp down the familiar impulse to reach for my reckoner. For some reason, I don't want it to capture her words. It would sully her and her story somehow, when I would much rather have this moment in my heart and mind to hold onto instead.

"Once, a young maiden with no family or friends cast herself from a cliff to end her suffering. But the stars sent the wind to catch her. Shaken, the girl walked until she found a road. The road led her to another town where she was turned away from every house. Disheartened, when she reached the banks of a river, she threw herself down on the rocks below. But the stars sent a wave to reach up and carry her over the rocks. It swept her far away until it finally relinquished her on a strange beach in another land.

"An old woman found her there and gave her a home. For the first time, the girl knew love, all the more precious for having been denied it so long. For many years, all was well until the old woman became sick. The girl did all she could to help her friend, but nothing worked.

"The girl railed at the stars. Why did they bring her here if it just led to more sorrow? At first there was no answer. Then the brightest star in the sky spoke, telling her this was the way of the world, a cycle of life and death, joy and sorrow. But the stars denied the girl death twice now. Why not interfere again?

"All you can do is take her place, the stars told the young maiden. She agreed, glad to pay the debt for borrowed time, and as soon as the words were spoken, the old woman woke and found the unconscious girl bathed in starlight. The girl died a few days later in the old woman's arms. Her sprit left her body and joined the stars in a brilliant new pattern that comforted the old woman in her loss until the day she too would join the stars."

Mother falls silent, the air around us weighted with the story. Finally, she clears her throat. "The Joyful One reminds us that we face many trials in life without knowing why. That there can be joy in sacrifice."

A lucerva yeanling squawks, and Mother laughs. "There's also joy in a long day's rest. We'll reach Miravat by dawn tomorrow."

Inevitably, my gaze goes to the Glass City, and it looks back.

The reckoner said it doesn't spy on me for the Provider, but I've kept it wrapped in hide and out of sight ever since I reached my mother in

Astrava. Now I pull it out of my pack. The device is slightly scuffed by grit and sand from our travels, but the screen still flashes in recognition when I speak to it. "Where can I enter the city without alerting the Provider?"

"That is a difficult question to answer quickly."

Beside me, Mother eyes the device with distaste but says nothing as we march. Dawn's not far off, nor is the Glass City. When the reckoner has no answer for me, I wrap it back up with a heavy sigh and return it to my pack.

"They won't welcome us at the gates," Mother says quietly.

"No, they won't." I try to recall what I can of the city's layout. A star flickers overhead, then it's gone in the receding dark. The last one we'll see for a long while. "Follow the Najimov. Miravat crouches over it like a brooding lucerva. That'll be your way in. I'll meet you there."

Mother nods at me. "I'm proud of you, daughter."

A tangled snarl of emotion closes my throat. I tried to do what she asked of me and failed when faced with the life I found in the Glass City. But I couldn't turn my back on everything she taught me. "Even though I disobeyed you?" I ask carefully.

"There are exceptions to every rule. Not everyone has the wit and strength to recognize them, however."

"Astravans have always been exceptional."

A soft smile curves across her face. "Yes, we have. Even as we wane, we shine."

While I stay the course toward the city gates, Mother directs the herd east along the river with Rakravat and Linarv's help. I've already shed my lucerva cloak and redonned my worn Miravat attire. The reckoner negotiates my entry with the liaisons guarding the city. It's simple enough to say I found difficulties in the desert. It's not even a lie. The liaisons may as well be made of stone for all the reaction they make as the gates are raised to admit me.

Breath sputtering in my chest at my daring, I cross the city, moving past quiet buildings full of Miravat residents who've yet to greet the day. The reckoner directs me down the twisting streets until I reach a small square. The Najimov, not much wider than it is in Astrava, cuts through it. A footbridge links one side of the city to the other. Metal railings keep people from getting too close to the water and the manicured plants growing along the riverbank.

I return the reckoner to my pack and shrug into my lucerva cloak. Let no one mistake me for a Miravat citizen today. Then I duck under the railing and scale the steep riverbank to the city's perimeter wall. An arched opening spans the river, bordered by a treacherous footpath on either side. Mother and the others are already lined up, the lucerva impatient for rest after the evening's march. A metal grate prevents them from entering.

I raise my staff and slam it against the top-most bracket anchoring it to the wall. On the third strike, the metal gives way with a groan. The second set of brackets crumbles even faster with the pressure of the river sensing an outlet after being pent-up so long.

The grate finally crashes into the water and slips out of sight. Mother leads the lucerva into the Glass City to the music of the Najimov. Linarv and Rakravat curse and cajole the animals forward along the rocky path. I scramble back up to the street and help guide the lucerva under the railing.

With unfamiliar stone under hoof, the lucerva pick their way awkwardly, then with greater confidence. As they do whenever they return to the pens in Astrava after each graze, they spread out, testing the limits of their enclosure. One of the males pokes his head through the doorway of a woman's shop on street level. She screams and slams her door shut. A trio of yeanlings scampers over the footbridge and onto the eastern side of the river. Another pair ventures down one of the side streets converging on the square.

Shrieks soon follow from the people of Miravat going about their morning only to come face-to-face with the creatures. Nearly half the herd still waits their turn to scamper up the banks of the Najimov and join the others. Linarv and Rakravat are sweating as they haul the rest of the animals into the street.

Mother watches the Miravat residents retreat in sneezes and panicked shouts. "You said the people here feared the lucerva."

"They do." Screams further out echo toward us. How can she doubt it?

She points her staff toward a woman across the plaza slumped against a bench, her hand pressed against her chest as she labors to breathe. "That's not fear. *That's* something else."

I look away guiltily from the woman's sickeningly pale face. *Right is not always easy.* "Don't remove your lucerva cloak, no matter what," I say in a hard voice, channeling the marking stone in my pocket, "and no one will dare touch you."

"What haven't you told me, Thurava?" Mother demands.

With a bray and a snort of indignation, the last lucerva is pulled onto the street. Linarv wipes his hands off on his tunic while Rakravat stretches out his back. "What now?" Linarv asks.

"We drive the animals into every part of the city," I answer.

The men spread out, tapping their staffs, but Mother doesn't move. "Thurava, I asked you a question."

I finally face her. "The people of Miravat fear the lucerva. Not simply because they are strange beasts, but because the animals make them sick."

Her brows furrow. "Like a poison?"

"All I know is it's something we Astravans can tolerate, but the Miravat cannot since the Great Scatter."

Mother looks like she did the time an ornery male kicked her in the stomach. I grip her sleeve. "We're the dying star blazing to glory. That's what you taught me. Whether it's sneezes, superstition, or something else, what we're doing this day won't be forgotten."

Mother slowly nods, a grim cast to her mouth. "May the stars bless us, for no one here will."

With that, we force the lucerva in all directions. Eyes wide and rolling with fear, people part before them, pushing and shoving in their haste to avoid the animals. With anger burning in my heart, I drive the animals forward. I don't dare look at a man who falls to his knees wheezing as we march by. Or a young boy who slams into the wall and passes out as the crowd seethes and roils around us.

I hunger to see the city dismantled and all the Provider's plans dashed to pieces. My gut burns with the years of deception that have hobbled Astrava. The people of Miravat need to bear witness to the evil they have gathered to them and given a home.

The first liaison I run across is stationed near the factory district. Before it can reach me, the fleeing crowd knocks it down, and its overlarge head separates from its spindly metal skeleton with a wave of sparks. The lucerva won't affect the liaisons, nor the Provider itself, but at least they can take away their living tools that have been turned against us for far too long.

We leave no part of Miravat untouched. As we make our approach to the upper city, wealthy residents keep their windows shut, but their faces press against the glass, horror in their eyes. One of the yeanlings in my group squawks, and the sound sends contractions of fear through the people hurrying away from us. A liaison tries to go against the current, but it's knocked aside. Metal gears whine as it tries and fails to right itself. Good riddance.

When we reach the first intersection, I send Rakravat and Linarv in opposite directions, their staffs driving half the herd along with them. At the next street, Mother breaks off with more of the animals preceding her, their ears pricked forward, curious at such a departure from routine.

With the last of the lucerva escorting me, I reach the plaza at the heart of the city. The people of Miravat have disappeared down side streets or taken refuge in houses and shops. I turn about the manicured green, uncomfortable with the hunger inside me demanding *more*. Always that. We've taught the Miravat a harsh lesson this day, but I cannot forget they aren't the only source of corruption in this city.

Two liaisons stalk toward me. One of the animals bleats mournfully as it's unceremoniously pushed out of the way. "Thurava, daughter of Sitarva, what have you done?"

I square my shoulders, stare into the closest liaison's face, trying to see past the blank visage to the Provider lurking underneath. "What I must."

The liaisons take up position on either side of me. I'm forced to leave my flock at the plaza as the liaisons lead me into the library and down the stone steps, not stopping until we reach the muggy chamber housing the artifact from the age before that dares call itself the Provider.

There, the liaisons both face me, speaking at the same time. It feels like a shout. "Thurava, daughter of Sitarva, by allowing the lucerva to enter Miravat, you have broken the law. What do you have to say for your actions?"

"Greatness has a cost. That's what you taught me."

"Cuckoo chick, you were given a gift. We remade you in our own image, and this is how you repay us?"

"You lied to us. Astrava's problems begin and end with you."

"You do not have the capacity to see your position in the world. How small you are in the pattern. A dying star, to put it in terms you can understand."

"Dying stars can still be beautiful. And deadly. You underestimated us."

A rumble thunders through the building. Steam billows, and I resist the urge to wipe condensation off my brow. I won't show weakness. I'm a blazing star.

The liaisons break off, each of their heads cocked. "You have incapacitated enough of my children to destabilize the city." They speak together still, but now out of step with one another, like an echo. "Ignorant child, do you not see the damage you have wrought?"

Mother and the others must have succeeded in their task. I must not fail in mine. "This is the only way for Astrava to shine to the fullest after you closed off all our other options."

"Your religion corrupts everything it touches," the left liaison spits out as the right cocks its head again as though listening to something only it can hear. "We should not have tried to save your people."

"Save us? You would gather us up just like he with the hunger that has no name and let us waste away in the stomach that is this city. Now, you will *choke* on us."

I swing my staff at the wall of pipes and gauges that power the city thanks to the Najimov's borrowed strength. The wood creaks upon impact, steam explodes into the room, and a high-pitched whine transforms into a groan as the wall buckles and bleeds water. A metal pipe flies through the air and strikes one of the liaisons, ripping the left arm from its socket.

"No. Stop. This is unacceptaaaaaaaaaaa . . . " The damaged liaison shudders and goes still.

Water roars and swirls around my ankles, crawling up my legs. It licks and laps at the base of the artifact, filling the room with a metallic-tasting fog.

Another rumble wracks the building. I slog toward the stairway. The remaining liaison flails after me. A spindly hand yanks me back by my pack. I splash down and go under. Lights and heat and water, all converging as the Najimov pounds into the room. Kicking up and away, I surface, gasping in deep lungfuls of acrid smoke.

"Thurava, daughter of Sitarva, you know not what you do. We have watched you grow, no matter how well-guarded by your mother. Quick to learn, ever curious about the world around you, compared to your peers." The liaison speaks with great effort as it struggles to keep its head above water. "We could teach you so much, help you rebuild Miravat—this time with the stars as our guide."

"I want *nothing* you have touched." I claw my way to the stairwell. Water already floods the first four steps. I get my knees under me and strip off my waterlogged cloak and pack so they can no longer weigh me down.

"You will change your mind. Now that you have seen what is possible, you will hunger for it. Whenever your mind is at rest, whenever you close your eyes, the Provider will be waiting."

Like the rotted seedpods of our grain? "*No*. You lie."

"I have never lied to you, child," the liaison practically spits. Its head cants up at an impossible angle to escape the rising water. "Better you to harness the possibilities I can provide to heal the city than someone else. Someone who will—"

The liaison sinks down, bubbles and sparks breaching the surface in its wake.

I scramble up the rest of the steps, fueled by the fury burning low in my gut, and return to the plaza. More liaisons have gathered, facing off with Mother, Rakravat, and Linarv. Lucerva are everywhere. Some gambol, jumping off benches or splashing in the fountain. Others try to eat the plants from the raised beds lining the plaza. Two yeanlings have curled up together, drowsing in the sun. Mother's in a heated exchange with the liaisons, but I'm too far away to make out what they're saying.

As I approach, a collective shudder goes through the assembled liaisons and, as one, they collapse, their limbs askew and still where they land, their metal skeletons splayed across the stone tiles.

Mother faces me. "What happened?"

"I freed the Najimov. The Provider's schemes can no longer hurt us."

She gives me a bow worthy of an Astravan elder. "May the stars make it so."

The liaisons stopped working that day and remained silent even after the artifact room in the library was drained. In the days that follow, we gather up the herd and keep the animals confined to the upper plaza. The people of Miravat have to be coaxed out of hiding by those originally from Astrava or Karnez. Some still sick, others merely sick with fear at the creatures that have conquered their city.

Mother vows to return the lucerva to the desert once a new treaty's brokered to prevent such a thing from happening again. The most high, the remaining members of Miravat's human council, and the clan leaders of Karnez meet for many days and nights until an agreement can be reached.

Of most importance, the Najimov and the underground river will run free for the benefit of all our peoples. An exchange between the different cultures will now be ongoing to heal the rift after years of distrust and reluctant trade borne out of desperation. Separation has made us all vulnerable, as the Provider demonstrated. In addition, every liaison and reckoner must be smelted down by Miravat craftsmen. Never again can we allow something we don't understand come between us.

Some welcome the changes, others mourn them, but for once all are in agreement the only way forward is together. I hope that will continue once the lucerva return to their home in the desert.

I've taken to spending much of my time in my room on the top floor of the Astrava lodge, uncomfortable with going about Miravat's streets while everything's so unsettled. Too many citizens now recognize me, my staff, and what I did. Even the common room is no refuge from the uncertainty my actions have created for everyone else.

But at least from my room's window, I can see where the Najimov flooded the streets, scattering refuse and bits of the broken city in its rush to return to its natural course and damaging the fragile structures that were built so hastily at the Provider's behest. Miravat's much changed, that much is true, but that only seems to improve it in my mind, since it's no longer pretending to be what it's not.

Someone knocks, and I open the door to find Kikriva staring back at me. I brace myself for whatever she's going to say—our last conversation still weighs heavily on me. She takes one look at my face and bundles me into her arms.

Numbly, I pat her shoulder and slowly extricate myself. "Kikriva?"

When she pulls away, she's crying. "I'm so sorry, Thurava."

"What for?"

"Because I didn't listen. I should have been there with you, by your side, when all this happened."

I expected anger from her, not regret. "What do you mean? You had responsibilities here." She told me as much.

She waves that off. "I thought that was the only way forward. It was all I could see for myself. But now, knowing the Provider's plots against Astrava . . . " She hunches her shoulders.

"Kikriva . . . "

"No. Let me say this." She takes a deep breath, gathering herself. "I never sent you any messages, Thurava. Not a single one. At first it was because it took so long to get settled. I kept telling myself I would contact you after things got better for us. But days then weeks passed and . . . they never did."

"I only wanted to know if you were well. The details never mattered to me."

A silent sob shudders through her. "Still. With the way we left Astrava, I so wanted to be able to tell you how wonderful life in the city was, but I couldn't bear lying to you."

"So you chose silence instead?"

She gives me a miserable nod.

So the Provider didn't keep Kikriva's messages from me as there were none to hide. Was that true of everyone else who made such promises? Their embarrassment at their changed circumstances in Miravat overriding everything else?

*I have never lied to you, child.*

"You were right that day about my work for Devanettu," Kikriva continues. "It wasn't what I'd hoped for myself, but it was the best I could manage here."

"There's no shame in that."

"But I still feel like a failure."

"Then that makes two of us."

Her eyes widen. "What do you mean? You finally made this city atone for how many years of injustice?"

"And what of the human cost of that?" For some citizens, their reaction to the lucerva's presence in the city was too extreme or medical care came too late. Their deaths are my fault. "What of me? My thoughts were only of my family, then revenge against those that would have Astrava fall." I hug my arms to my chest. "Before I learned of the Provider, I'd almost convinced myself *I* was a discordant note in this city, having failed to find my place within it."

Kikriva shakes her head. "You shine wherever you go. Never stop, Thurava."

I hope that will be enough, I think to myself when Kikriva takes her leave. Those early days after the Provider's fall, the lodge had to be guarded against angry citizens once they learned of my involvement. I still have much to account for.

Mother finds me later that day in my room. She pulls my pack from behind her back and lays it on the bed. It must have been recovered when the artifact room was cleaned out. "Well? Have you made your decision?"

I turn away from the window and sigh. "I wish none of this had happened, that Astrava had never been threatened, and I never came to this place. Then I wouldn't hesitate to return with you to the herd."

So many people have to rebuild their lives, and I feel responsible for them all.

"You'll find your way. In this, and everything else."

"But how? I don't even know how to choose my path forward."

"Then don't choose. Do both. Stay here and learn. When you're ready, you'll know how to find us. The lucerva are still your birthright." She presses a kiss to my brow. "Shine brightly, little one."

When she leaves, I pick up my pack, thinking to move it out of the way, but its heaviness surprises me. I pour the contents onto my bed. My lucerva cloak, a roughspun tunic, a small clay vessel full of vitav salve, and a hide-wrapped package. My reckoner. I forgot about it while the rest of the city renounced theirs.

I slowly ease back the flap covering the screen. It flashes. "What can I help you with, Thurava, daughter of Sitarva?"

With a yelp, I wrap it back up. I should get rid of the thing once and for all. I hold it to my chest. All I have to do is walk downstairs and see it done. But the knowledge it contains, not only of the city but that of my own people and our stories of the stars . . . A gnawing ache blooms inside me as I hesitate, curiosity warring with what I've promised—what we've *all* promised.

Is this the hunger that has no name? A desire for more? Even if I don't know what that really means? Or perhaps my time in Miravat has changed me, clinging to what might one day be of use.

In the end, I bury the reckoner in the bottom of my pack and place the whole thing underneath the bed. I'll be strong enough to withstand the temptation it represents, I tell myself. Prudent to keep it safe, though, in case we ever have need of it to help heal all the damage that's been done. And better me than someone else.

After all, the Provider has never lied to me.

## END

# ACKNOWLEDGEMENTS

*A Hunger With No Name* was written primarily in and around Albuquerque, New Mexico, on the traditional, unceded territory of the Tiwa people. I moved here in 2009 with my family, and I hope you can feel my love for the high desert on every page of Thurava's story.

Sometime in 2016, the inspiration for the Glass City came to me in a dream. I had envisioned a young woman staring off into the distance, the horizon shimmering in a strangely menacing way. I didn't understand why, only knew that the sight was both beautifully compulsive and a threat to the land surrounding this solitary figure. The next day, I started writing a short story that swiftly grew into a much longer one, trying to put into words what I had dreamt and what it signified. Over the course of many months and years, on a journey that would daunt even the Great Navigator, the story eventually evolved into the novella you see here.

I am greatly indebted to my friends and colleagues who helped me refine this story along the way: L. Blankenship, Sarah Burr, Christopher East, Nicole Feldl, Chris Gerwell, Jennifer Grimaldi, Kelly Lagor, Lori M. Lee, Emily Mah, the late John Jos. Miller, Sara A. Mueller, M.T. Reiten, Laura Snapp, the late Janet Stirling, S.M. Stirling, Sarena Ulibarri, Sandra Wickham, and Fran Wilde.

I am also grateful to the team at University of Tampa Press for taking such care during the book's publication: Dr. Julie Nelson, Wesley Kapp, Yuly Restrepo, Madeline M. Eisele, Daleyna Abril, and Anika Schmid.

My writing would not be possible without the support of my family. My husband Eric is my first reader and my forever home. My daughter Brynn inspires me each day to be a better version of myself. You will always have my love and gratitude.

Lastly, I am thankful to you, reader, for the time you have spent with my words.

May the stars shine down on all of you.

# ABOUT THE AUTHOR

Lauren C. Teffeau was born and raised on the East Coast, educated in the South, employed in the Midwest, and now lives and dreams in the high desert of New Mexico. When she was younger, she poked around in the back of wardrobes, tried to walk through mirrors, and always kept an eye out for secret passages, fairy rings, and messages from aliens. She was disappointed. Now, she writes to cope with her ordinary existence. Her novel *Implanted* (2018, Angry Robot), mashing up cyberpunk, solarpunk, adventure, and romance, was shortlisted for the 2019 Compton Crook award for best first SF/F/H novel and named a definitive work of climate fiction by Grist. Her short fiction can be found a variety of professional and semi-pro speculative fiction magazines and anthologies. In addition to a bachelor's degree in English, she also holds a master's degree in Mass Communication and spent a few years toiling as a researcher in academia. To learn more, please visit http://laurencteffeau.com.

# ABOUT THE BOOK

*A Hunger With No Name* is set in Garamond Premier Pro digital fonts, based on original metal types by Claude Garamond and Robert Granjon that were designed and cast in Paris, France, in the sixteenth century. The book was designed and typeset by Wesley Kapp at the University of Tampa Press. The cover was designed by Madeline M. Eisele.

www.ingramcontent.com/pod-product-compliance
Lightning Source LLC
Chambersburg PA
CBHW020154120726
47903CB00007B/2557